One Shot to the Heart of A Gangsta 2

D'Artanya

Sydney

The back of the police car was like a prison in itself. The seats had to be made of the same shit as the red and yellow Little Tike cars. My hands being tied behind my back wasn't how I imagined my first experience with handcuffs. I'd pictured furry restraints against a man's headboard.

The police didn't strap me under the seatbelt; I thought they were being kind. They weren't. Every turn was wide and fast. Unable to use my hands, I was forced to use my abdominal muscles to keep my body from shifting around with the car. It felt like I was doing crunches.

I was grateful to arrive at the station. The officers yanked me from the car and pushed me when I wasn't walking fast enough. Still, it was better than the ride there.

I thought I met the peak of my embarrassment in court with Kyle. But when the officers had me strip down to nothing, my cheeks went hot. Bending over, spreading my cheeks, and coughing had to be the pinnacle.

"The videos on pornhub are far better," one of the arresting officers joked.

I cringed at the violating remarks of my body. The purpose was to break me down before my mugshots. It didn't work. My mugshots were pageant worthy. It was giving damsel in distress. And I was.

After the check-in process, I was taken to a holding cell. I sat at the the center bench, back against the wall, holding myself because I was freezing.

I was fine the first hour because I was alone. It wasn't long before there were three other girls in the holding cell with me. Apparently, they'd gotten into a fight at a concert. Why they put them in the same cell, I didn't know.

"Your fat ass always doing something, Iesha, damn."

"Reka, I'm trying to tell you," she punched her hand into her open hand. "Call me fat again and I'm gon' fuck you up," Iesha responded, mushing Reka against the bars of the cell. The lock hit her back, and she screamed in pain.

"Look at this little fancy bitch right here." The mannish looking one scooted closer to me. "I'm Domo. How you doing?" She held her hand out.

I looked at her hand like it was diseased.

"Bitch, don't look at my girlfriend like that. She said hi; speak the fuck back!" Reka yelled at me. "You shouldn't be speaking to these bitches anyway!" She punched Domo in her arm.

"Yo. We not together." She slapped her hand with each word. "You broke up with me. This morning in fact." Domo shook her head at Reka.

"It was an argument, Domo! I didn't mean it. Just like you didn't mean what you said to me!" Reka was panicked.

I remembered that feeling every time Kyle threatened to leave me. What a fucking joke that turned out to be. If she knew what I knew, she'd get far away from this Domo girl.

"What I ain't mean?" Domo twisted her lips. Iesha and I laughed.

"Something funny?" Reka's neck snapped in my direction.

Everyone was laughing. I didn't know why she focused on me.

"Bitch, I said was something funny?" She walked over to me.

I stood up. I'd never been in a fight in my life, but she looked liked she was about to hit me. Staying seated didn't seem like the smart decision.

"Oh, you want to fight?" Reka was so close, I could feel her breath on me.

"The girl clearly don't want to fight. Leave her the fuck alone!" Domo defended me.

"You tryna play hero so you can fuck her later?" Reka suggested.

"Why you so concerned with who I put the strap on? Your bird ass won't be getting it no more. Like I told you earlier, go find you a dick to spin on, you for play play lesbian."

Everyone laughed again and I swear, this time, I tried to hold my laugh in, but I couldn't help myself.

"Ms. Sharpe!" The guard called my name. "Looks like your lawyer is here."

I watched him walk to unlock the gate and started towards him when my body went tumbling to the floor.

Reka kicked me. I grabbed ahold of her leg and pulled her to the floor with me. It did nothing to stop her. She landed two hits to my face before the guard pulled her off of me.

I was thankful to him because those two hits were enough for me to not want more. He walked me out to the front, and I saw my father. In a rush to get to him, I walked faster than the guard, and he yanked me backwards. I watched my father's jaw clench as I was uncuffed.

"If you ever yank my daughter like that again, I will kill you and represent myself to ensure I beat the charge." My father had his finger on his chest. Let's go, Sydney."

I rushed to my father's side, grabbing his hand as he walked me out of the doors.

"What happened to your face?" he asked, stopping just outside the precinct doors.

"I think I got into a fight." I kept us moving to the car.

"What's the little bitch's name?"

"Daddy, please. I just want to go home."

"If it was up to me, you would've been in boxing classes when you were four," he shook his head, unlocking the car doors.

I climbed in, slamming the door.

"Aye, now. I know the first time getting your ass whipped hurts, but my car ain't do it. Don't be slamming my doors." He started the engine.

"I don't care about that. I was arrested for murder!"

My father waved me off. "That shit ain't nothing to stress about. It was just a little payback for Kyle. That's how the system works behind the scenes. It's unsolved, and it will stay unsolved. You shouldn't have any more issues out of them."

I didn't know what he was talking about, but I knew he knew what he was talking about when it came to this legal stuff, so I trusted him.

I pulled down the visor and looked at my face in the mirror. "Oh, my God! What am I supposed to do about my face? Makeup can't hide this." I touched it and flinched.

"A little red meat will get you right. Don't worry about it."

How could I not worry about it? My eye was going to be a dark purple by the time the sun rose. Juice was supposed to be taking me on a real date this week. I couldn't go looking like target practice.

"Aye, listen. I know you're still upset with your mom, but I think nursing you back to health is right up her alley. I'm sure she'd love to see you."

He had a point. She'd have me looking like myself again in no time. I felt a little shitty for going off on her and now needing her. I never said I wouldn't need her, though.

"Yeah. I think I'll stay with her until I'm feeling a little better."

It wasn't long before my father pulled into the driveway. I was surprised to see my car there.

"How'd my car get here?" I asked my father.

"I'm not sure, baby, ask your mother."

"Ok." He walked around to the passenger side of the car and opened my door. "Thank you, Daddy."

"Anytime." He grabbed my hand, helping me out. "Call me if she drives you too crazy or you just miss your pops." He smirked before getting back in the car. "I love you!" he said before shutting the car door.

"I love you, too."

I took a deep breath, preparing myself for the over exaggeration of my mother when she saw my eye. She was going to lose her shit, threatening to sue the city and anyone else she felt was responsible.

My mother gasped when she saw me, clutching her chest.

"Whew. You scared me. I wasn't expecting you to be home." She buried her face back into her laptop, laughing.

"Um. Excuse me," I pointed to my eye.

"Oh, my God!" Her hands shot up to her mouth. "Is it ok if I get you some ice?" she asked.

"I just had ice; it needs heat now," I rolled my eyes, sitting down.

I was more than a little annoyed that she didn't notice my eye until I pointed it out to her. She was supposed to back off a little, not completely ignore me.

"Ok. Do you want to tell me what happened?"

"Why are you being so weird?" This was not the mother I was used to.

"I've been meeting with a support group for smothering mothers. I've learned a few things. The most important thing I've learned is that I should ask permission before I do any type of prying. You're a person, not an object I can manipulate however I want."

"I'm not a social experiment that you can try your tricks out on either." I folded my arms across my chest.

"Sydney." My mother put her hands to her head. "I'm trying. I would love to be all up in your space and your business, but you don't like that. So, I'm trying to do things a new way. Please don't make me feel like I'm not doing enough. How about this, you tell me what you need, and I'll make it happen?"

I nodded my head. "A hug." My eyes watered.

My mother rushed over to me, wrapping her arms around me. I needed my smotherer just a little longer.

Carnage

Josie took the fuck off. Pops was forreal when he said she was in training. I looked across the street to see her using the ledge of the neighbor's Koi pond to get over their fence. I ran across the street, following behind her. It'd been a while since I'd jumped a fence, but I did it with ease.

Josie was frozen in place. A Rottweiler was barking wildly at us being in his yard. She was terrified of dogs.

"So, I guess you have to talk to me now. Or at least listen to what I have to say."

"Shut the fuck up, Carnage. I'm trying to think," Josie rolled her eyes.

I wasn't bothered by the dog. I could jump back over the fence. She wasn't getting over without me giving her a boost.

"The only way out is back over the fence. I'll help you over *after* we talk."

"I don't want to fucking talk," Josie said through gritted teeth.

"That chain don't look like it's going to hold him much longer," I warned her.

"Fine! Say what you gotta say."

"I read the journal. Pops wasn't who we thought he was."

"So, she fucking kills him! None of us are who we say we are. We trick people into thinking we're someone else. That's the fucking job!"

"Shit is not that simple, Josie." I slapped the back of my hand into my palm. "You keep saying you ready to be in the field, catching bodies, but you too fucking emotional!"

"I know I'm emotional, but I don't act off of my emotions."

I twisted my neck, pointing to the Rot that was trying its hardest to get off the chain.

"This is different," she sucked her teeth. "I'm smart, Carnage. Maybe I'm not ready to kill as efficiently as you do, but I can do that shit," she pleaded. "I know when I'm in danger, I have the gift of gab. Charm. And I'm not scared of shit except dogs. I can be really good."

I nodded my head, hearing her for the first time. "Maybe you jump in helping Shany for a few. Learning the intricacies of things from the inside." Josie pursed her lips. "Just until you learn it, then I promise, I'll show you how to take a nigga out myself," I tapped my chest.

"Ok, but I want to be in on everything. Stop keeping stuff from me. I want to be treated like an adult."

"You got it," I threw my hands up.

"What was in the journal?"

"Nia was my sister," I confessed.

Her mouth dropped. I didn't want to tell her, but I had to do whatever I had to do to calm her down.

She wiped her eyes and nodded her head. "Fuck him then."

"Fuck him."

"Now, get me back over this fence before this dog fucking eats me."

We laughed as I gave her a boost to the other side of the fence before hopping over myself.

"So, I guess that means you're in charge now?" Josie wrapped my arm around her shoulder as we walked back to the house.

"I guess so." I didn't even think about that part. My first concern was getting to my sister.

"I'm in charge of the business and the family." She looked up at me.

"Yeah. I got you." I kissed her forehead.

We walked into the house to find my mother, standing in the same spot I left her in.

Josie exhaled. "I'll take her in the room." She walked ahead of me, reaching her arms out to my mother. "Come on, Mommy." She held our mother's hand as she stepped over my father's body.

When they cleared the room, I texted Shany.

Is Tiana sleeping?"

I stood over his body, looking for any sign of life. His eyes were wide open. I wasn't going to try and save him; I was going to finish the job. I planned to make him pass down the entire company to me. Now, I didn't have to because it all belonged to me.

Yea

As I was walking to Shany's room, her door opened. I stopped walking when I saw her face. She tried to move past me, and I stopped her.

"Before you go out there—"

"If it's not my mother, I'm fine," she said, moving past me

to see our father laying on the floor. "You did this?" She checked his neck for a pulse.

"Mommy." I ran my hands down my face.

Shany nodded her head. "I don't need to know what was in the journal. I see what the shit has done to everyone else. Did he deserve it?" she asked, closing his eyes.

"I don't know," I shrugged. "I'm not his maker."

"Would I have done this to him?" she asked, finally moving away from his body.

I nodded my head, certain that if she saw our father grabbing me up like that, she would've shot him.

Shany pulled her phone from her basketball shorts. She dialed a number and placed the phone face down on the table. She pushed her AirPod into her ear. "Yeah. I need a cleaner." Shany gave the address before ending the call with a hard press to her AirPod.

"Twenty minutes," she said, grabbing a water from the fridge. She leaned against the kitchen island. I sat on the arm of the couch.

"Did it take long for Tiana to go back to sleep?"

"No. I told her it was just a nightmare," Shany shrugged. The way that girl was screaming for her father, I almost thought you were," Shany laughed. "I can tell she loves you. Relies on you like the rest of us. I guess she isn't so bad. I can deal with a niece. I'd be a dope ass auntie." The both of us burst into laughter.

My mind was racing with the things I wanted to do with Essex Elite. I wanted to add a new service. A division responsible for street justice. For the women who weren't successful in getting restraining orders from abusive exes. For the children who were harmed and stuck in foster care system. For the patients who couldn't sue hospitals for the addictions they created. For the deserving. It wouldn't make us any money, but it was possible it could wash some of the blood from our hands. I wasn't tryna be a superhero. Being the villain was rewarding.

Shany went over to the door, holding it open. A sexy ass model looking bitch walked in, looking like she was here for a nasty girl photoshoot. She wore a black leather jumpsuit and some black-on-black stilettos. She carried a matching leather bag that looked like it was an overnight bag. With black latex gloves, she pulled cleaning supplies from her bag, placing them on the kitchen island. Her hair was in a top knot bun, with her edges laid to perfection. No makeup, no lashes, no jewelry, and the bitch was bad as fuck. If she didn't work for me, I'd put her in my pussy budget.

"Yo, Shany. Why the fuck you got these bitches—" The girl eyed me like she wanted to cut me. "Women. My bad. Why you got these women cleaning bodies looking like sex vixens?" I twisted my head.

"She bad as fuck, right?" Shany laughed.

"Cleaning is such an ugly job. I feel sexy when I'm cleaning up crime scenes. I usually go straight home and fuck my dude," the model girl spoke as she ran water into a black bucket she pulled from her duffle bag.

Her heels clicked around as she moved. The switch was turning me on.

"Yeah, well, take them fucking shoes off. That shit mad loud." I mugged her before going to check on my mother and Josie.

I couldn't watch her clean and not want to fuck her. After seeing pen to paper of my father's secrets, I would never be the nigga to fuck an employee. Wouldn't none of these bitches be comfortable with me.

I placed two soft knocks to my mother's door before walking in. Josie had her finger up to her mouth as she rubbed our mother's head. Our mother laid in her lap, crying in her sleep. I leaned against the door, just watching the two of them. All of the women in this house were now my responsibility, including the one in the living room who thought she was a boy. Tiana had to be above the rest because I had a duty to her. I snatched her mother from her and placed her in an unknown environment. I wanted all of this shit I planned to work out, but if it didn't, I'd move on to the next thing. But when it came to Tiana, I refused to fail at that.

I thought with a promotion, I'd have the time I needed to love on Sydney the way I wanted to. The way she deserved to be loved by a man. All the promotion did was dump more on to my lap. It felt like I would never get back to her. I thought to call her since we exchanged numbers, but if my sisters thought I had a girlfriend, they'd never shut up about it. I made a promise to call her whenever I made it back to my own damn house.

I refused to get out of bed at the sound of my phone ringing. Someone would have to physically remove me from this pillow if they wanted me up. When the ringing stopped, I snuggled further into the covers, ready to doze back off. The phone immediately started ringing again.

"Ugh!" I threw my covers back. I sat up in the bed, rubbing the crust from my eyes. "Shit!" I forgot my eye was fucked up.

"You ok, honey?" My mother knocked at my door. That had never happened without a jiggle of my door handle immediately after.

"I'm fine. Thank you!" I called out to her.

The second I stood out of the bed, my phone stopped ringing. I was already up, so I slid into my slippers to start the day. My phone started ringing again, and I looked around for it. I couldn't find it to save my life. When I remembered my father said it was in my purse, I rushed over to it, only for it to stop ringing again. It was Ayanna calling me nonstop. Before I got the chance to call her back, she was calling again.

I answered the FaceTime. "Why are you calling me like a crazy person?" I carried the phone into the bathroom with me to wash my face.

"Ooh, friend." Ayanna scrunched her face up. Who did that to your face?"

"A bitch I met in jail," I shrugged.

"Well, we can go find her, because she fucked you up."

I mean mugged her in the camera. "She only hit me twice."

"Well, she landed them motherfuckers well."

"Ayanna, please!" I shook my hands up and down in frustration.

"Ok, ok, my bad. Was that your first fight?"

"Did you call for something?" I sucked my teeth. I added hot water to my rag — as hot as I could stand it — and began to clean my face.

"Oh, yeah. How do you get released and not call anyone to say you're out?!" Ayanna yelled.

"I was tired. I came home and got straight in the bed," I shrugged her off. I carefully rubbed in the creases of my bad eye.

"So! You let people know you're ok. We made sure your car was back home, and I used Google to find your father's number to tell him you were arrested. I was connected to some rude ass old lady who couldn't pronounce my name for shit. You could've at least sent a text, Syd." Ayanna shook her head at me.

My father picked me up and dropped me off with my mother — the only two people who were required to know my whereabouts. I hadn't considered letting anyone else know. It hadn't crossed my mind that they would be concerned about me.

"Sorry. I've never been *released* before. I don't know how none of this shit works," I bit my lip.

"Well, for future reference, call someone."

"No need because I don't plan on ever being in handcuffs again." I carried the phone in the kitchen to get my breakfast.

"Juice been in his head, worried about you, girl. The nigga acting like you gave him some pussy or something." I smirked.

"Wait. Did you?"

"No," I laughed. "It's just nice to be thought about." I looked around the kitchen, not seeing a single piece of ready made food available. "Let me call you back." I pressed the red button before she could argue.

I knocked on my mother's door and walked into her room at the same time. She was on her bed, eating a bowl of oatmeal with her laptop in front of her.

"You didn't make me anything?" I asked, confused.

"I didn't. I'm sorry," she twisted her lips. "I can get you something."

"It's fine." I left her room, allowing her door to slam behind me.

This was some bullshit. I came here to be catered to, not to be treated like the red headed stepchild. I sent my father a text saying that I wanted to come home with him. He sent a text back saying that I was more than welcome to stay at the house while he was in California for the weekend.

I just wanted to be loved on. I scrolled my contacts, waiting for my bagel to finish. I deleted Kyle and his friends, realizing I'd never taken the time to. J's name was bundled with Jemma and Kyle's. I thought to call him, but a FaceTime from Juice popped up on my phone.

I watched it ring, debating on whether to answer or let him hang up. I wanted J, but he wasn't here. He had my number, and he wasn't calling me, Juice was. At this point, J was just a fantasy. Juice was ready and willing to make my reality as beautiful as the fantasy I was holding in my head. I didn't want Juice to see me like this either, but the fact that he hadn't given up yet and was letting the phone ring, in hopes of talking to me, made me want to answer. I settled on answering, rushing to click the button, now anxious to talk to him.

"Hey?" I gave a small smile. I knew he would notice my eye, but I was hoping he wouldn't focused on it.

"What's up, Jail bird Barbie? Damn. What happened to your eye?"

I smushed my lips together. "Bye."

"My bad, my bad." He held his hand out as if he could reach up and prevent me from hanging up. "It just caught me off guard is all. You still beautiful, Barbie."

"Thank you." I tried to hide my smile but to no avail.

"Welcome. What you doing tonight, though?! I owe you a date." He spit sunflower seeds into the street.

"Not like this. I look a mess." I moved away from the phone to pull my bagel from the toaster.

"That ass still perfect."

When I realized he was talking about my actual ass, I giggled like a schoolgirl. He didn't miss a beat with the compliments.

"Where you trying to go? I don't want to be all dressed up in a fancy restaurant, ordering a steak that should be on my face instead of a plate." I spread cream cheese on my bagel.

"We can save the make up for another date. We can go to Waffle House or something where it's no big deal to see a girl with a black eye."

"Waffle House?" I scrunched my face up.

"You don't like Waffle House?"

"I've never been. There's always a large crowd and to be honest, it doesn't look very clean. I usually ride past." I licked the cream cheese from the knife.

"Yeah, we definitely fitna get your black card black. So,

check it. Maybe we can slide to the movies beforehand.

"Or, you can come to my place until then." I bit into my bagel. "Well, not my place but where I stay when I'm with my dad. He went back to California for a few days, so I have the place to myself."

"Long as he don't come home with a gun, I'm down. Shoot me the address, aight? Later, beat up-Barbie." My mouth hung open in shock at his new spin on my Barbie name. "I couldn't help it." He threw his arms up, and I hung up on him.

I wanted to be mad, but I found myself laughing at it, too. I got my ass beat. I took another bite of my bagel with a dumb grin on my face. My phone chimed with a text from Juice.

You still going to send me the address, right? I was just playing.

I was going to send it to him, but not without making him sweat a little first.

∞ ∞ ∞

I chose a taupe short set with an off the shoulder top. My hair was slick into a long, flowing ponytail. I kept my makeup light, settling for lashes, light mascara, and lip gloss. Butterflies made their way to my stomach as I waited for Juice to knock on the door. He told me he was outside and on his way up; I was expecting him any second now.

I jumped when I heard the knocks. "Calm down, Sydney," I whispered aloud to myself. I wiped my hands down my thighs before getting up to open the door.

"Hey," I smiled nervously.

"What's up, Barbie?" Juice pulled me into him for a hug.

He placed a kissed to my lips before stepping inside. He stood in place, waiting for me to shut the door.

"This place is dope. This your pops's crib?" he asked, following me to the couch.

"Yeah. Temporary place. He lives in California. He came to help me with my court stuff, then I begged him to stay a little longer," I smirked, picking up the remote from the coffee table.

It was awkward sitting next to him on the couch. I felt like I should say something, but I didn't know what to say.

"You want to find something to watch?" I offered him the remote. If it was up to me, we'd be watching *Grey's Anatomy*.

"Nah, put *Friday* on."

"Ooh, it just started, too." I turned it on and made myself comfy next to Juice. "I'm excited the see what all the hype is about." I put my throw over the lower half of my body.

"Wait," Juice laughed. "You've never seen *Friday*?"

"Nope. Shut up so I can watch it."

I'd never seen it. There were a lot of black classics my father had been trying to convince me to watch, but I kept turning him down. He was going to have a fit if he found out I was watching *Friday* without him.

"That's wild."

It was never a big deal that I hadn't seen the black classics when I was with Kyle. There was no humiliation or pressure about it. It wasn't a big deal to me. Now that I was surrounding myself with people who looked like me, I was excited to be in on the cultural secrets I wasn't familiar with. I'd understand the random movie references that didn't make a lick of sense to me before.

"I can smoke in here?" Juice asked.

"Yeah," I nodded.

My father would not be okay with that shit, but he wouldn't be home for a few more days, and the smell would be gone by then.

Juice rolled the blunt, and it was hard for me not to stare at his lips while he spun the blunt against his tongue. God, how I wanted to be a blackwood. Once he lit the blunt, I snuggled under his arm. He held the weed to my lips three times before I decided I'd had enough.

It didn't take long for me to be invested into the movie. I laughed so hard that my eyes watered. I couldn't help but notice the glances Juice kept taking at me. I wasn't sure if he didn't like my laugh, or the shit wasn't funny, and I was just high.

"Something wrong?" I asked.

"Nah. Why, what's up?"

"You keep peeking at me like I'm doing something wrong."

"Nah. I keep looking at you, wondering if you could do any wrong." Juice stared into my eyes, and my body warmed at his words.

I nodded, having nothing to say and focused my attention back on the movie. Juice was looking like a good replacement to the fantasy I was holding for J.

When the movie ended, I was ready to eat, but Juice wanted to smoke one more time. I suggested the balcony because I was trying my father by letting Juice smoke the first time. We walked outside, holding hands, with me leading the way.

I leaned against the railing with my shoulders as Juice lit his blunt. He came up behind me, resting his weight against my body.

"You sexy as fuck," he whispered in my ear before turning

my face to his. He exhaled his smoke into a kiss that made me want to hand my body over to him.

"Thank you," I whispered.

He took a seat in the chair and pulled me face forward on to his lap. His frame was big. I felt tiny nestled onto his lap. Juice put the blunt to my lips and I inhaled. When I began to blow it out, he pulled me into a kiss. It turned me on. I found myself grinding on to his lap and moaning into his mouth as he had a strong grip on my ponytail.

He moved his hands beneath my dress. I allowed his hands to find their way to my pussy. Full on eye contact, his fingers went in and out of me, until my body began to shake.

"Can I have you?" Juice whispered into my ear and made my pussy pulsate.

I nodded my head, rushing to pull him from his jeans. He let the spit in his mouth serve as lube for his dick before pulling a condom from his pocket and sliding it on. A little nastier than I went for, but if I didn't have to suck dick, I wouldn't complain.

I lifted my leg a little to get him in me. He bit my lip as he pushed himself fully into me. I forgot how to breathe. Juice used his left hand to hold my back up while using the right to play with my clit. I was losing my grip on reality as my closed eyes and colored stars came my way.

Juice picked up his pace. I swear I felt my pussy rearranging, but the pain felt good. He pumped as deep as he could go. I still wanted more of him. We weren't close enough. I wanted to be in his skin.

"Give me that shit," he growled, fucking me harder.

I nodded my head. "Don't stop. Harder." He could rip my shit apart, and I wouldn't complain. "Hurt me," I begged him. He moved his hand from my clit and used both hands to force me onto it like I was one of those pocket pussies for his enjoyment. I loved every minute of it. "Oh my God. I'm cumming," I called out. He bit down on my nipple as I came all over him, whining in pleasure.

I thought we were done. He'd have to get his another time because my body had nothing left to give. He stood me up, moving my body to the ledge of the balcony. Juice bent me over the railing and delivered pumps into me with force. I loved it. I threw it back on him, wanting him to fuck me stronger, deeper, but he couldn't handle it.

"Woah, woah, woah." Juice wrapped a hand around my stomach and kissed down my back to settle himself. "Slow down. You gon' make me cum."

I stopped throwing it at him and let him rejuvenate inside of me.

"I knew you'd feel like money, but money never felt so good." He slowly worked himself in and out of me. "You not going to be able to get rid of me." He kissed me one last time before pumping deep into me, finding a rhythm. The breeze that graced the crack of my ass, set me off. I bucked on him wildly, until he began letting out high-pitched moans, unable to announce he was cumming. Three strong pumps and he was done. He pulled out of me, throwing the condom in the small trash can on the balcony. He pulled my dress down and relit his weed.

The rest of the time on the balcony was silent. Our bodies stayed connected like we were made that way. The breeze blew, sending a warmth through my body. Post nut clarity, I immediately regretted giving him some. He felt good. He felt right. But I'd felt all of this before. I wanted to be sure before I gave myself to another man.

When his blunt was finished, I let him drive my car to take us to the Waffle House. He tested its limits, almost hitting a hundred on the freeway. In the Waffle House parking lot, I felt like we were at a club. There were people everywhere. Music blasted from different cars, but it was all overpowered by conversations circulating the parking lot.

Juice opened my door. We held hands for the walk inside. Every person in the parking lot stopped to speak to him. We kept walking, but he spoke or gave a head nod. I felt like a celebrity walking inside the Waffle House. We ordered our food and went to wait by the car. He leaned against the car and placed me in front of him. Hugged up on the car, I felt like the Bey to his Jay-Z.

"Hey, Juice." A cute light skinned girl rubbed his shoulder, walking backwards, licking her lips as if I wasn't fucking standing there.

"That's an ex of yours?" I asked him, never taking my eyes off of her. I wanted to remember her face, in case I ever saw her again.

"Something like that," Juice said, kissing my shoulder.

"What does that mean?"

"I used to put dick in her," he lifted. "Get in the car. I'm going to get our food. We can eat at your people's house."

I got in the car like he said. I appreciated him telling the truth, but that didn't mean I trusted him. I watched him walk inside to grab our food and come back to the car, making sure he didn't stop to hold a conversation with the girl. He said nothing to her. A few handshakes were had on his way back to the car before he got in, and we pulled out of the parking lot.

Carnage

I was ready to take my ass home, but my mother wasn't having it. Every time I tried to leave, she'd almost be in tears about me taking Tiana home. She didn't give a fuck if I left, but Tiana was the only thing giving her joy at the moment. I didn't want to leave without Tiana because I needed her for my comfort, too.

I was laying across the couch, holding the pillow against my head with my hand, with the remote in the other arm that was stretched out. The doorbell rang, and I didn't budge.

Josie came out of the room and sucked her teeth. "When are you going home again?" she mumbled. I didn't bother to answer her but looked towards the door to see who it was.

"Camille. This is not the best ti—" Josie started to speak, but Camille cut her off.

"I'm aware. I'm here for Carnage." Camille moved around the house like she was apart of the family.

She sort of was. Camille was my father's assistant. She was the one with the FBI connect. It was a move she made on her own. Came to us with all the shit we needed. She kept dude in her pocket and whenever we needed some info, she tossed him a little pussy. I didn't know what the fuck she was here for, though.

"What you looking for me for?" I raised my eyebrows.

"Because you're the new boss, and there's a warehouse full

of people waiting on orders." She said it like I should've known.

"I keep forgetting I'm in charge now. I'll do that shit tomorrow," I shrugged.

"No. You'll do it now. People have kids to feed. It's not a well you can turn on and off. Throw something decent on, and I'll be in the car." She switched away from me.

"So, you going?" Josie asked me.

"It doesn't sound like I have a fucking choice." I got off the couch.

Being in my father's position, I thought I would be able to move the way I wanted. I was still taking orders _ and from an assistant at that. She was my assistant now, and I should've been giving her orders instead of being ordered around like a worker.

After a shower, I tossed some shit on and met Camille in the car.

"So, I need your schedule as far out as it goes. I need every contact in your phone to be sent to me. Tiana. What are we doing about her?"

"She's not a problem you have to worry about juggling. She's my responsibility. How the fuck do you even know about her anyway?" I cut my eyes at Camille. She was already doing too much. The mere mention of my daughter made me question her.

"I knew when they reported that a body was found in a nearby body of water, and not in the same place with her mother and grandfather, it wasn't her body. You had that body placed in the water to make it look like her. X had already prepared me to have her executed upon sight but_"

"Bitch, I will kill you dead."

Camille just looked at me. "*But* I wasn't in agreeance and now that he's gone, I no longer have to. You're my boss now. The duties I was carrying out for X, trickle down to you. I will focus on whatever you need me to focus on." She glanced at my dick.

"And if I'd prefer to find my own assistant?"

"You can do whatever you'd like, but know that I will *not* be training someone to take my job. You can spend your time, money, and resources to teach her how to work for you. I, on the other hand, already know what's required of you, while you haven't figured it out yet. Like, we're pulling up in front of a warehouse with workers wanting to know where their boss is. Do you have an answer prepared?"

"Imma tell them motherfuckers he gone," I shrugged. "Let them know it could be them if they step out of line."

That wasn't a big deal. Yeah, some of them had been in the game far longer than me, but if X taught me anything, it was that I wasn't scared of shit. I could kill anything that had a pulse.

"That won't work with this group of people. They aren't concerned with dying. They don't fear that. They fear that you won't be able to keep up with X. They're worried that the empire will fall with a new King. They're most concerned with feeding their families. You have to go in there and show them that you can do the job better than your father. If not, you may not have a team of workers anymore."

I nodded my head. I expected more time to come up with a speech I could give these people but no sooner than Camille finished her sentence, the car parked in front of a warehouse.

"I hope you're ready." Camille got out of the car, not bothering to wait for me.

I didn't like nothing about any of this shit. Camille was letting this shit go to her head. She was about four years older than me, and it felt like she was tryna carry me like I was a little nigga.

"Come on," she said, opening the door and walking in without me.

I kept at my own pace. I wasn't the type of man to run after anything. If it didn't come to me on its own, it'd have to wait until I got to it. I grabbed the handle of the door and walked into a room full of fucking people. I recognized a few faces, but most I'd never seen before. When I counted cleaners, hitmen, undercovers, and all the other little shit, there were well over a hundred people in the room. I guessed it was one of those see it to believe type of things.

"Ladies and gentlemen—" Camille started to speak, and I stepped forward, cutting her off.

"Good afternoon. I looked around the room, trying to make eye contact with every single person in the room. It was impossible, but I attempted. "Those of you who don't know me, I'm Carnage. If you didn't know, I'm the only son of the now deceased X. No need to offer your condolences because I don't give a fuck." I looked around for any reactions that didn't sit well, but they gave nothing, or I saw nothing.

"I'm not interested in downsizing or getting rid of anyone that's already a member of Essex Elite. I'm actually looking to expand. I want to add a service. Street Justice. Pervert who gets off, the DMV worker making shit complicated for the everyday man, that CEO who treats his employees like shit, the husband who beats his wife and then sleeps peacefully because she's too scared to press charges," I shrugged. "If you're interested, send your ID in an email. If you have a name you'd like to add to the list, add your ID number twice. Someone will reach out to you to get the information needed for the kill. I prefer it not be personal, as you should be handling that for yourself, but for serious offenses, I'll make the exception. Any questions about any of what I just said?" I looked around the room for a raised hand or someone standing, and there was nothing.

"Moving on then. Any grievances with the way my father ran things? Something you would like to see change? You have my undivided attention. I'd rather we handle it now so that my father's beefs are not being handed down along with his business." I laughed and a few chuckles went around the room.

A woman in a church hat stood up.

"Yes ma'am." I leaned against the tables, crossing my legs at the ankles and holding my hands out in front of me.

"There should be job availability. I have grandchildren now. I'd prefer not to be undercover for long periods of time. I know I signed up for this life, but life changes. Circumstances change and I would like to change with it."

"So, you want to do jobs but not long-term jobs?"

"Exactly."

"Anyone else agree with that?"

Enough hands raised for me to make it happen. "Camille, is it possible that we post jobs on an app similar to the one truckers use to find loads? Maybe even have an entire dispatch setup?" I turned to her.

"It will take time, it will cost money, but we can definitely get that done. I like that idea." She wrote some shit down on a notepad.

"So, we'll work on that," I nodded my head, and she took a seat, smiling. "Next?" I looked around the room, and a man in the very last row stood up.

"I want to see how much a client pays versus how much I made from it. X was taking fifty percent. I don't think that's right. We're the ones putting our freedom and lives on the line."

A few people in the room expressed their concerns from their chair.

"I feel you, but Essex Elite pays for transportation, hotel stays, vehicles, weapons, cleaners to clean up your mess, and a shit load of other shit." I counted out each item on my fingers. "Not to mention the fact that the work comes through us."

"I get that, but I can clean my own crime scenes." Dude put his hand on his chest.

"And that takes jobs from us," one of the cleaners stood up. "That's not fair. Everyone has a job to do."

"I don't give a fuck about what's fair to you. I have a family to feed. I'm concerned with my table and my table only."

"Everybody, relax. With the added street justice service, there will be plenty of cleaning jobs to go around. You will be taken care of. That's a promise."

The girl nodded, taking a seat.

"As far as your concerns, I hear you. Fifty percent is a lot. So, those of you who are willing to clean your own crime scene, to Essex Elite standards, can receive sixty percent of the job fee. The street justice jobs will be listed on the app as bonuses. You will keep a hundred percent of the fee that is listed, but you will provide your own means of transportation, goods, etc." I looked to Camille. "Are you writing all this down?"

"Got it." She never bothered to look up from her notepad.

I looked back at the man with the money concern. "I met you halfway. Are we good?" I spread my arms wide.

"Yes, sir." He sat down, satisfied.

It was three hours before Camille and I were able to wrap up the meeting. It wasn't how I planned to spend my day, but we got some shit done. I felt like Essex Elite was off to a good start under my command. Some well needed changes were underway, and the staff left feeling better about who they were working for.

It was a win for everyone, except my stomach, because I was starving. Camille drove us to Popeyes. We went through the drive thru and ate in the parking lot and talked.

"I think you did great in there. You're filling your father's shoes well."

"Thank you, but I'm not trying to fill his shoes. I'm trying to create my own path. Fuck that nigga." I downed some lemonade to get the dry ass biscuit residue from my throat.

"Can I ask why you killed him?" Camille wiped her mouth with a napkin.

"I didn't." I gave her a cold stare that let her know she need not ask anymore questions about my father's death. She nodded her head, accepting what I said.

"Before I drop you off, let's go through this calendar." She took a sip from her straw before pulling her iPad out.

As we were leaving the warehouse, Camille had me AirDrop my calendar and my contacts. I kept eating as she went over everything. My calendar was pretty much empty because I completed the last job I had scheduled.

"Calendar looks good. Vancouver Island is a nice vacation. I've only been once, but I had a great time." She took a sip of her drink. "Let me see the contacts." She scrolled through the names. "So, I'm familiar with all of these names except one."

I knew what one she was referring to without seeing it because outside of Sydney, everyone in my phone was family or business.

"Sydney." I nodded my head.

"Who is she?"

"A friend. That Vancouver Island trip you saw in my calendar is to see her." I bit into a thigh.

"Sounds like more than a friend."

"Sounds like it ain't your business." I wiped my mouth with a napkin.

"My job fully involves looking out for your well-being. So, it sounds like Sydney is a woman who occupies your mind if you have planned a trip to see her three months in advance." She twisted her lips and rolled her eyes.

"What's your point?" I took another gulp of lemonade.

"My point is, a man in your position cannot maintain an outside relationship that's not work related because then, you'd have to be three people—Carnage, whoever you are to Sydney, and whoever you are on whatever job you're on. Two is enough for the best of the best. I'm not saying you can't be with this Sydney girl, but what I'm saying is, if you want to be with her, she has to come to your world."

I nodded my head. Camille wasn't telling me anything I didn't already know. Either way, I was going to get my girl once I got all this shit in order. Although, she hadn't called or texted me, and for her to have begged for my number then not reach out was weird. I was hoping she hadn't moved on from me yet. I needed her to know I was coming soon.

Sydney

Three Months Later

"I love you," Juice said, kissing my cheek.

"I love you, too," I lied.

I thought I loved him, but the last month of this bullshit relationship had been just that— bullshit. It may have taken me a while, but I was familiar with all the fucking lingo now and knew why they called him Juice. All the niggas wanted to be him, and all the bitches wanted to be on his arm. He claimed he kept the hoes in line and only allowed them to suck his dick from time to time because I wouldn't anymore. It only took one bitch to throw a sub at me on social media for me to never put my mouth on his penis again. Two months in, we stopped using condoms but after that incident, we were back on them. He'd tried sneaking it off, and I ended the entire session. He'd take his ass to the bathroom and jerk off or go for a ride, which really meant he was going to see another bitch.

Three months ago, I had my first fight. In that little bit of time, I was on my sixth fight with only one loss. The one I took in jail that day. I only needed to get my ass beat once to know I would never let it happen again. They always went for my face. I still didn't know how to fight, but I picked up whatever was closest to me. The last bitch I chased down with my car. She was so tired from running, I was able to fuck her up with ease. I said I was never going to let a man change me again, and I was doing the shit again.

"Then why you won't give me none?"

"Because I'm not in the mood," I shrugged.

"I'm not trying to hear that shit, man. Because if I go outside and get some pussy, you going to be out here, hitting bitches with bats and shit."

"You act as if I'm just being an unnecessary bitch or something!" I screamed, getting out of the bed. "All you do is fuck other bitches. Why would I want you touching me? How the fuck am I supposed to get in the mood? I look at you and all I see is the bitches I've had to beat the fuck up over you. It's not me! It's you, and my body is not interested. What the fuck do you want me to do?"

"Control your body instead of letting it control you, like an adult."

"You got a lot of motherfucking nerve, my nigga." I punched my hand into my fist. "How 'bout you control your body, and we wouldn't be in this predicament in the first place."

"When the fuck are we going to move past that?"

"We could if you would stop putting your dick in everything, but you can't." I laid back down, getting comfortable under the covers.

I wore an oversized T-shirt with the words *Sleeping Barbie* on them. Juice had gotten me a whole set of them. Before, I wore them because I was proud that he'd made the effort. Now, I wore them because they were comfortable.

"Man, I don't have time for this shit. I'll be back." Juice got out of the bed and left.

I wanted to be done with his ass. I left him twice already, but every time, Ayanna would call and tell me how sad Juice was. Most of my time was spent as his place, alone. My father was back on his overworking shit and at his house, I felt lonely.

At Juice's place, I enjoyed the alone time. It was usually party central in this motherfucker. I could've gone home with my mom but if I was being honest, I was attached to Juice.

I thought of calling Carnage so many times, but the fact that he hadn't called me in all this time, held me back. It wouldn't surprise me if he'd found someone he was ready to settle down with. I mean, I had Juice, so I couldn't be upset. I just hoped that whoever the woman was, Carnage didn't think she was better than me.

Like clockwork, Ayanna was calling my phone.

"Yeah?" I answered, already knowing what she wanted. It was always the same thing.

"What happened, Sydney?" Ayanna asked.

"Don't know what you're talking about," I yawned, in need of a nap.

"Juice called me, cursing and hollering like he and I are beefing. He said y'all keep having the same argument. You're still not fucking him? Syd? What do you think he's going to do?"

"I don't care what he does anymore, Ayanna. He's already shown that he's going to do it anyway. When I caught him cheating the first time, I was giving him pussy damn near every day, sometimes twice a day. It still didn't stop him from campaigning for the community. I'm not the one he wants. It doesn't matter if I was perfect; I don't fucking do it for him. I've accepted it and I'm done trying. So, you can tell him that he can go fuck who he wants, because I don't care anymore."

"Why are you giving me attitude? I didn't do it."

"Because you're supposed to be my friend. You're always calling me when we get into it, trying to make me forgive him, understand him. When do you have time to help him understand me? Are you giving him the real like you claim to be giving me? I know you knew him first, and he's like family to you, but I should be important, too. You should be speaking to him in my defense the same way you call to tell me about how he's feeling," I ranted.

"First of all, I curse his ass the fuck out, frequently. I don't let him slide about shit. Second of all, I just want y'all to stay together. He loves you and is acting out because he doesn't want to be in love again. You just have to wait a little longer. I promise, the nigga you want is in there."

"I'm tired of being patient, Ayanna. I'm over his ass."

"What about our road trip? We leave in five days, Sydney. You're just not going now? He's going to be so annoying, crying about you not being there," Ayanna whined.

"I agreed to this trip two months ago, *before* he started cheating on me. I don't want to go anymore."

"Please, Sydney. After the trip, if you want to break up with him, cool, but please don't ruin it for the rest of us. Don't make us have to deal with him like that. I am begging you."

"I'll think about it. I have to go." I hung up before she could say another word.

I had plans with J in five days. I fully intended to leave J hanging a month ago, but now that Juice and I weren't on good terms, I was reconsidering.

"Oh my God, I can't breathe!" The bitch underneath me gasped for air.

Her head hung off the bed, and I stood over her piledriving my dick into the back of her throat. I held her neck up with my hand, making sure she didn't hurt herself.

"You want me to stop?" I asked.

"No, I want more."

I forced myself back into her throat. "You like that shit, don't you?" I let her catch her breath.

"I love it." She played with her pussy as I shoved my dick back into her throat.

The bitch had one of the prettiest pussies I'd ever seen. Naked, plump pussy lips that covered her clit almost perfectly until it began to swell. If this weren't a job, I'd suck on them until she exploded. I wasn't here for that, though.

"Bend over. Let me put this dick in you." I stepped out of the way for her to lift up. Her face was covered in spit. While that wasn't typically my thing, she looked damn good. She was turned on by it, and that had me ready to go.

She put her head down on the bed and spread her ass cheeks. I swiped my dick up and down her crack before sliding into her. All power strokes into her juice box. She moaned like I wasn't giving her the best dick of her life, but I wasn't giving her my all. I slid a finger into her ass to make sure she could handle what I came for. She went crazy for it, and I knew she was ready. I slid out of her, and I watched her eyes water as she begged for me to fuck her.

Fucking her was payback to her husband, but I didn't want to hurt her. I slid my dick into her ass slowly. When she threw it back, taking it all like a Hungry Hippo, I almost fell back. She flexed her walls around my dick. I pounded into her like I was in some pussy. Her moans turned into a sound I'd only heard from wild animals as she came on my dick.

Wasn't shit sexy about it, and I went soft. She'd already gotten her nut, so I pulled out of her. She fell out on to the bed while I zipped my jeans up.

I turned around, yanking the tape from her husband's mouth.

"Ahh, fuck!" he screamed, bouncing around in the chair he was tied to. A few of his mustache hairs were stuck to the tape.

"Make better choices," I said to him before walking out of their room.

"I'm going to find you, nigga. Believe that!" he barked at me in anger. "Get your thot ass over here and untie me, bitch!" he yelled to his girl.

There weren't too many threats I took seriously. Put me next to whomever, and I was still at the top of the food chain. There was something about his tone that made me believe him. I pulled my gun from my hip, turning back into their bedroom. I took one shot to his head. His neck dropped and blood poured from his head and onto his lap.

His bitch didn't flinch. She sat there, mouth hanging open. I searched her face for relief, fear, something that would help me decide if it was okay to let her live. She gave me nothing. So, I shot her. One in the head.

As I walked down the steps, I marked the street justice job as done. I didn't know what he did, but it was in the app with a 5K payout. It wasn't far from the crib, and it'd been a minute since I'd been in some pussy. I hadn't planned for it to turn into a murder scene, but it was what it was.

While in the app, I created a job for two cleaners with the address and state of the dead bodies. I waited for the job to be accepted before pulling off of the block.

The five stacks I made to fuck the bitch was paid out to the cleaners. So, I spent five thousand on some less than extravagant pussy. I was more sexually frustrated than when I started the job.

The trip I promised Sydney was coming up, and I still hadn't heard from her. To be fair, I hadn't hit her up either, but she was the one who'd asked for us to exchange numbers. I thought she would've hit me up by now. It had me thinking that she was preoccupied with another nigga.

My call to Camille rang throughout the sync of the car.

"Hello?"

"What's up? You busy?"

"I'm always busy. What you need?" Camille asked.

"That trip to Vancouver Island, I need you to cancel it."

"Why? You've been turning down all this pussy I've been throwing at you because of this girl. Now you want to cancel the flight to see her? Make it make sense."

Camille had been offering me all kinds of pussy — before work pussy, car ride pussy, after work pussy. I wasn't clear on if she just wanted to fuck *me* that bad, or if she just wanted to be fucked in general. Either way, I wasn't going for it. If the sex was bad, it would complicate things. If the sex was good, it would *really* complicate things. She was bad, though. If I were a weaker nigga, I'd hit.

"For once, can you just do what I asked without a million questions after?"

"Carnage. You bought a whole ring for her. Been talking all this shit about proposing, so if you want me to cancel the date with the love of your life, I need a good reason."

It was an irrational decision I made during a trip to the mall with Tiana and my mother. I roamed the jewelry store while they did their thing. My focus was on a new watch, but the perfect ring was blinging in the corner of my eye. I asked to see it, immediately pictured it on Sydney's hand, and that was all she wrote. I wasn't sure I was ready to jump right in to being a husband, but I *was* ready to jump into the deep end with Sydney. Eighteen thousand dollars on a ring she would never see because I wasn't going to Vancouver Island.

"You know you work for me, right?"

"I work *with* you to make your life the best that it can be. If you're not going to propose in Vancouver Island, then come to the lakehouse with me instead. You can meet the family and everything." Camille sounded sarcastic, but she was being serious.

"I'll think about it. Just cancel the flight, please."

"Please and thank you are the magic words. I think it's a bad idea, but if that's what you want, I got you."

"Thank you."

"You're welcome. Let me get back to my business. Later." Camille ended the call.

I wanted to see Sydney, but my pride wouldn't be able to handle it if I showed up and she didn't.

Local kills were far and few in between. On the rare

occasion that I killed some shit close to home, I stopped by Oneisha's crib. Oneisha was a girl I used to hit when I was in high school. We stopped fucking because she fell in love with some new to the hood ass nigga and wanted to be faithful. I respected it.

Dude ended up doing her dirty and leaving her down bad with a baby. I always had love for her, and I had the money to help her. I got her a car and gave her the money to get in her own spot. She kept talking about repaying me. She didn't have it and I didn't know when she would. I told her I'd continue to pay her rent for however long as long as I could use her spot for cleanup. I could shower, change clothes, and she'd toss the old clothes out with her regular trash. She agreed.

I texted her while I was waiting for the cleaners. She responded saying cool, but when I was at the door, she was slow as fuck letting me in. It was the first time in all these years that I had to use my key. When I opened the door, I saw why.

It was early evening, but you wouldn't be able to tell. The curtains were closed, and the lights were off.

"Yo, what the fuck is this shit?" I stretched my arms out, looking at the trash around the apartment. Nesha moved around in the dark.

My feet weren't touching the floor. Instead, I was stepping on empty chip bags, candy wrappers, and pizza boxes. I tried to flip the light switch and got nothing.

"You got Ariel in here with no lights?" Ariel was my goddaughter.

"I lost my job," Nesha cried.

"How long ago?"

"Three months." She wiped her face.

I was paying all of the bills. When she got herself a little job, she insisted on taking care of something. We agreed on the light bill.

"If you been home for three fucking months, why this shit look like this?"

"I was trying to clean it, Carnage, I just—"

"Clean it how, Nesh?! You need a professional service for this shit." I kicked shit out of my way as I stepped.

I led myself into the kitchen to find worse. The sink was piled high with dishes, the counter was covered with used pots, pans, and silverware. The roaches didn't bother trying to scatter.

"I'm sorry —"

"What the fuck is all this noise out here?" I heard a nigga's voice.

I could feel my blood pressure rise as I followed the voice. A scrawny ass nigga barely above five feet, stood in the living room, one sock on, one sock off, scratching his balls.

"Who is this nigga?" I used my thumb to direct her eyes to him. He was opening the blinds, so I guess he had some sense. Nesha was in the light now, and I could see bruises all over her body. "Is this nigga hitting you?"

The Nesha I knew would never let a nigga put his hands on her — especially not no bitch ass nigga like that one.

"My boyfriend," Nesha stuttered. "No, he's not."

"Wh-who the fuck is you?" He scratched his head. "This my shit!"

"Your shit," I laughed.

In one motion, I pulled my gun, shooting him in his head. All the while, my eyes never left Nesha's.

"Are you using?" I asked her, lifting her chin, ignoring the silent screams.

She shook her head no. "Then what the fuck is wrong with you?" I twisted my neck. "Where the fuck is Ariel?" I asked about her daughter.

"At my mother's for the weekend." She was on the floor, holding her knees, as I walked back and forth.

"Good. I should have this shit cleaned up by the time she gets back. Nesha, listen to me. When this shit is cleaned, keep it the fuck clean. The next time I come in this bitch and find trash like that, you going out with it."

I wasn't going to be able to clean myself here until my cleaners cleaned this bitch up. I put in a request, offering an extra five stacks for the domestic shit that was beneath them. My cleaners weren't fucking maids. Nesha had me hot. Apartment managers could put you out for being a dirty bitch. I guess she didn't know that part.

Something told me to check the bathroom, her bedroom, and Ariel's bedroom. The bathroom smelled like a sewer. It looked like it hadn't been cleaned in at least a year. "I should fuck you up, you know that?!" I yelled, coming out of the bathroom. I didn't bother to check her room. I went straight to Ariel's room.

"Nesha!" I screamed. "I know you don't got her sleeping in this shit!" I slammed the door, rushing out to the living room where Nesha was.

"She sleeps in the living room most days," she winced, fearing I was going to hit her.

"You think this is any better? I grabbed her by her throat, slamming her against the wall. I squeezed tightly until I could feel her pulse in my hands. "You's a nasty ass bitch. You know that? I'm doing pop up visits from now on. I catch a single nigga in here, I will kill you and take Ariel from you. You here me? I will bury you six feet under, bitch!" I slammed her again before letting her fall from my hands. She flopped to the floor, grabbing her neck.

I knew the knock at the door was the cleaners. I let them in like I lived there. "This shit fucked up, seriously. Throw all this shit away — dishes, clothes, if it can move, it's in the trash."

"Carnage," Nesha whimpered. "What am I supposed to do without anything? Ariel can't live like that."

"But you thought it was cool for her to be in this fucking mess?" I twisted my neck at her, and she put her head down. "You'll get a delivery tomorrow. New everything. Nesha, if you don't take care of my—"

"I will," she nodded, wiping snot from her nose.

"Bitch, you better."

I walked out of the house, shooting Camille a text about what was needed for Nesha's place. I laughed in the car. I was fitna be running a daycare. Taking all these bitches' kids.

Sydney

Juice and I sat in a booth across from his mother and his stepfather. They were begging to go away with us this weekend. Juice refused and instead treated his parents to dinner. After dropping me and his mom off to her house, he and his father left for the sports bar. I wanted to be at home in bed. His mom insisted that we do our own thing, so I was stuck going with her to the Bingo Hall.

I didn't even want to go on the fucking trip with Juice, Ayanna, and their dusty ass crew. My insecurities wouldn't allow him to go without me, though. I'd already spent a significant amount of time considering that he could take someone else, meet someone there, or make a detour to meet up with one of the bitches I'd already beaten up. I wished I could get over his ass.

"Bingo! Haha!" His mother clapped her hands together with her tongue hanging out of her mouth.

I gathered our things, knowing that once she collected her winnings, we were out of here for the night. I shouldn't have been excited to leave because we were going to her house to sit on the porch while she played her casino games on her phone and smoked her cigarettes. Spending time with her made me miss my own mother, especially since she wasn't as overwhelming as she had been before. The only thing interesting about Juice's mom was the stories she shared about her childhood. It helped me understand why Juice was the way he was.

That was part of the reason it was so hard to leave him. I pitied him. He didn't even know who he was because his entire life, his mom had made all of his decisions — the same way her father had done her. His birth father wasn't around, and his stepfather chose to be one of his homeboys rather than the father figure he'd intended to be. He had the husband shit on lock, though, from what I saw, anyway.

"Whew!" His mom fanned her shirt. "I'm sorry, honey, but I got to turn this air on. Mama is hot!" She turned the air on.

"It's fine." I scrolled my phone, placing my free hand between my thighs in preparation of the air turning on.

"What's wrong with you?" she asked.

"Nothing. I'm fine."

"No, you ain't. It's my son, ain't it? Boy always doing something," she shook her head. "I don't know why you deal with him. You can have damn near any man you want, and you're wasting your time with my child, who don't give a damn about himself let alone anyone else."

"He cares about me. He just—"

"Has a funny way of showing it? Listen, the man for you won't have a hard time loving you, trusting you, and whatever else you're looking for, honey. Juice may care about you, but he's not ready to love you. He's still trying to figure out how to love himself. Don't spend so much time trying to teach him how to love that you forget how to love yourself."

"I hear you."

I'd already forgotten how to love myself. Again, I was lost in a man. It didn't matter how I felt about it because I was too far in to pull myself out of it.

"Oh, Lord. What is this girl doing here?" his mom mumbled, parking and rushing out of the car. "Give me a second."

I was right behind her. Juice's family was close, and I was certain I'd met them all, except the ones who lived out of state. So, whoever this bitch was, was a problem. I could feel it in my chest.

"Hey, ma!" the girl smiled, following Juice's mom up the front steps.

Ma? I was starting to think this was another one of Juice's bitches. She took a glance back at me but didn't say anything. When we made it up the steps and on the porch, I moved away from the steps. I stood in front of the patio set and introduced myself.

"Hi, I'm Sydney, Juice's girlfriend." I didn't bother to extend my hand for her to shake because I was preparing to swing on her.

"You can't be Juice's girlfriend. I'm his girlfriend and have been for years." She scrunched her face up at me before turning to his mother. "Ma, who is—"

I grabbed the glass ashtray and hit her across her eye mid-sentence. I couldn't fight to save my life, so I had to make use of the things around me, swing first, and make my hits count. That first hit forced her right eye closed. She tried to swing but couldn't get a good view. I swung the ashtray again, hitting her in her other eye.

"I can't fucking see!"

"Good!" I yelled before swinging the ashtray backwards to get my strongest hit to her face. My hand went too far back, and the ashtray cracked against the brick wall of the house. It didn't stop shit. I took the broken ashtray and made a strong swipe to her face.

"Sydney! Oh my God!" Juice's mom yelled.

I stopped swinging and stared at the girl bleeding onto

the green turf that covered the porch. There was no sadness or fear for what might happen to her. The only thing I felt was worthless. I was fighting over a nigga who had me fighting over him on his mama's porch. I grabbed my purse from the chair and began walking down the steps.

I walked down the street to the corner store, tucking the glass into the sewer before ordering a Lyft. The stupid niggas on the corner tried to holla at me. It was like they were oblivious to the sadness I knew was showing on my face. It didn't matter to them. It felt like I didn't matter to anyone anymore.

The Lyft dropped me off to my mom's with a ninety two dollar price tag. A total of one twenty if you counted the tip I left him. If he'd tried to kidnap me, I wasn't certain that I would've had the energy to fight him back, so the tip was a thank you for getting me home safely.

There was a car in front of our house that I didn't recognize. I wasn't in the mood for guests.

I used my key to walk into the house. It looked like I was interrupting a date. My mother and some stranger ass nigga were hella close on the couch.

"Ma, what's going on?" I flipped the light switch, stuffing my keys into my purse.

"Um, Sydney, this is Rodney," my mother stuttered as she spoke and scooted away from him.

"Hey, how are you doing?" Rodney stood and extended his hand.

"I'm fine. Nice to meet you." I gave a small smile before eyeing my mother like she'd done something wrong. I wasn't sure what I was upset about. What I did know was that I wanted to be with my mother. Just me and her. I needed my wounds licked like only a mother could do. Instead, she was trying to lick on this stranger in our living room.

"Rodney made us dinner," my mother beamed, holding a glass of wine. "There's some left over if you'd like some."

"No thanks," I shook my head, walking back out of the front door. I was headed to my father's condo, at least for the night.

I made it to my car and pulled out of the driveway. I was expecting for my mother to come running after me, but she never came. I drove slow to my father's house, hoping other plans would magically pop up. If I had any sense, I would've been on the plane that left this morning for Vancouver Island.

The low music cut off, as Ayanna's name popped up on the screen. I pressed ignore. When the sync switched back to my music, I turned it up, trying to fake a good vibe until one found me. I wasn't but two lines into some Summer Walker before the car sync was interrupted with another call from Ayanna.

"Yeah," I answered, merging onto the freeway.

"What the fuck, Sydney?"

"I don't want to hear it. Did you call Juice and ask him what the fuck?"

"Juice wasn't the one who stabbed somebody on his mother's porch!" Ayanna said, with a clenched jaw.

I sucked my teeth. "Nobody stabbed that girl. I swiped some glass across her face. It's hardly a stab wound," I rolled my eyes.

"Well, you cut her! Juice didn't do that. I called the right person because you did that, Sydney. What is wrong with you? What are you going to do if she presses charges?" Ayanna asked.

"Get my lawyer daddy to get me off. She don't have one of them. Dumb bitch probably doesn't even know who her father is! That's why she was willing to lose her life over that stupid ass nigga, Juice!" I screamed.

"Well, you have your mom and dad, so what does the fact

that you were willing to do the same over the *same* dumb nigga, say about you?"

"That I'm just as dumb as she is," I exhaled.

"Long as you know."

I didn't give a fuck if Ayanna was offended because that was what I thought of every female Juice dealt with behind my back. They were all beneath me. Most of them had their own nothing. The ones who had a little something had multiple kids. They held jobs but not careers. A good wig that they prolly stole from the hair store. And no sense of style, outside of what made their asses fatter and showed their titties off more. I was above that, and I didn't give a fuck how anybody felt about it. I was a top tier bitch, and he kept cheating on me with these bottom feeder bitches.

"Did you call for something?" I gave Ayanna attitude.

"We're supposed to be leaving in the morning, assuming you're not in cuffs by then. I was calling to suggest that you ride with us instead of Juice because I think it's best we keep the two of you separated.

"I would agree, but I'm not going. I'm done with Juice. And if you keep calling me to defend him, I'm going to be done with your ass, too."

Police lights flashed, and their sirens went off behind me in the middle of my rant. "I'm getting pulled over. I'll talk to you later." I ended the call with no intention of calling Ayanna back.

My heart was in my throat, thinking that I was on my way back to a fucking holding cell for a nigga I stopped caring about the second I left his mother's porch. My palms began to slip and slide on the steering wheel from the sweat building on my hands. My heart raced, watching the officer get out of his squad car.

When the officer made it to my car, I found out I was going ninety in a sixty-five. I hadn't realized I was speeding. Ayanna pissed me off. He let me off with a warning when I gave him my name. He could've just as easily been pulling me over for assault with a deadly weapon. I couldn't believe I did something so stupid. This was really a night from Hell.

I skipped the exit for my father's condo and pushed towards the airport. I could still make it if I caught the next flight out. I could go on a mini shopping spree and buy clothes while I was out there. At this point, I didn't care if J showed up or not. I needed a vacation.

"Daddy, daddy, daddy!" Tiana woke me up with hits to my body.

"Yeah, Ma Ma. What you need?" I rolled over to face her.

"It's time to go!" She pointed to the clock.

I looked at the clock. It was 7 a.m. I looked back to her to see she was fully dressed with her Crocs on and her book bag on the floor near the door.

"Where are we going?" I didn't know what she was talking about. I thought maybe I told her we were going somewhere and forgot about it.

"Auntie Camille said when the clock said seven, zero, zero, we had to go see grandma."

"What?" I scrunched my face.

She went to repeat herself, and I stopped her. I grabbed my phone and called Camille on speaker. She answered on the first ring.

"Hello?"

"Why am I going to my mother's house at seven a.m.?"

"To drop Tiana off," she said with a mouth full of food.

"And what am I dropping her off for?"

"So, you can go to Vancouver Island and get your girl. You better get up before you miss your flight," she smacked in my ear.

"The flight I told you to cancel?"

"I must've forgot."

"You ain't forget shit. Stop playing with me, Camille." I twisted my lips, while tickling Tiana, making her giggle.

"What's your point? Either you're going to get on the plane or not."

"I'm not." I hung up on her.

I stared in Tiana's face. She was enough for me. The more I stared at my daughter, the more I pictured our future. Tiana, me, and Sydney. Sydney was in every vision. I had to go get my girl.

I jumped out of bed, washed my face, and brushed my teeth. I tossed on an Amiri tee and a pair of jeans. "You ready, Ma Ma?" I asked, grabbing my keys from the dresser.

"Mmhmm." She reached her arms out for me to grab her off the bed.

"Let's go."

"Is we going to get on a plane, Daddy?" she asked, while rubbing my head.

"Soon, Ma Ma, soon." I bent down to grab her backpack as we headed out of the bedroom, then out of the front door.

I was going to get my baby on a plane soon because she would not stop harassing me about it. The entire car ride was filled questions about planes. I answered all of them like I was more interested in it than she was. My mind was on Sydney. I was going a little over the speed limit, anxious to get Tiana to my mom so I could get to Sydney.

When we pulled up, I carried Tiana out of the car and ran up my mom's steps two at a time. I used my key to get in the house. "Go find grandma." I put Tiana down on her feet.

"Ok." She ran off. "Grandma! I'm here!"

I found a seat at the kitchen island, searching my email for my boarding ticket. I didn't know what time the flight was or shit else. I heard the clicking and clacking of heels in the living room. I focused my attention on the doorway, waiting to see who was going to walk by. Josie's face dropped when we made eye contact.

"Sneaking out?" I asked, spinning in the stool.

"I'm grown; I don't have to sneak in or out," Josie rolled her eyes.

"I wasn't talking about you. I'm talking about whoever else is with you." A woman stepped forward, showing herself from the other side of the wall. She waved with a grin.

She was fine as fuck. Small enough for me to fling her around a bedroom. She ain't have much ass, but the titties were popping. Her lips were full and juicy.

"I'm Carnage," I stood, reaching my hand out. "Josie's older brother. You are?"

"Her gi—" She tried to speak, but Josie interrupted her.

"Don't talk to him." Josie dragged the girl away from me.

I laughed, throwing my arms up. "I'm just saying hello."

Josie kissed the girl before slamming the door in her face.

"You are so embarrassing!" Josie stormed over to me and pushed my chest. She got frustrated when my body didn't budge from her push.

"You better be grateful I'm laughing and not fucking you up." I went back to my seat. "Y'all know how I feel about having randoms in here."

"She's not any more of a random than Tiana." Josie went to

the window, watching her girl pull off.

"Tiana is blood." I raised an eyebrow.

"I don't care if it's the blood of Jesus, she's still a random."

"Ummm, I think I want oatmeal," I heard Tiana's voice.

Shany appeared with Tiana in her arms. Tiana ran her hair through Shany's dreads. It took all of two weeks for Shany to fall in love with Tiana after wanting nothing to do with her. They called each other best friend. My mother often called me when Shany was gone so I could bring Tiana over, and they could get some time alone.

"Don't you have a flight to catch?" Shany asked, sitting Tiana on the kitchen counter as she gathered the items for her oatmeal from the cabinets.

"Yeah, I was waiting to see Mommy to make sure she was cool with watching Tiana until I came back."

"I got her. She's with me all weekend. Right, girl?" Shany held her hand up, and Tiana gave her a five.

Shany was a big help. She did all the work to create Tiana Essex on paper. She had a birth certificate, social security card, and is set to start school this Monday. I was more nervous than both of them. Tiana had long stopped asking about her mother, but it only took one slip up. Just in case, we came up with a story of where her mother was. She dropped Tiana off at my door one day, and we hadn't seen her since.

"Yep. Daddy, it's me and my best friend all weekend. You can go back home now."

My mouth dropped at Tiana trying to get rid of me. My sisters laughed at me, with Josie laughing harder than I liked.

"I was on my way out the door, but Josie had a house guest. She tried to sneak her out, but she was clinking and clanking around the corner in those loud ass heels and shit," I laughed.

"Carnage, shut up!" she slapped my arm. "Damn."

"What kind of house guest?" Shany turned around. "A nigga?"

"A bitch."

"Daddy, you said a bad word," Tiana interjected, with her hands still in Shany's head.

"My bad. She had a very beautiful woman over here."

"So, are you finally coming out of the closet?" Shany asked, picking Tiana up from the counter and turning the pot of water on.

"I was never in the closet. I was minding my fucking business," Josie spat with an attitude.

"Ooh, Auntie Josie, you said a bad—"

"Shut up." Josie stuck her tongue out.

Shany carried Tiana over to her, and they started play swinging on her. "Tell her don't talk to you like that, best friend," Shany encouraged Tiana, as she was still swinging her tiny arms at Josie.

"Don't be talking to me like that." Her neck twirled as she spoke.

"Aye! That's enough, man. Turn that hood shit down a notch. She starts school soon. We don't need them issues."

"If she starts school on Monday, why are you going out of town?" Josie asked.

"I'll be back to see her off for her first day. Mind your business," I scrunched my face, pulling my ringing phone from my pocket. "Yeah, Camille," I stood from the chair.

"You better be on your way to the airport."

"I'm walking out of the door as I speak."

I gave Tiana and both of my sisters a kiss before rushing out of the front door. I was using them as a distraction from the butterflies building in my stomach, knowing I was about to see Sydney in a few hours. I felt like a bitch ass nigga forreal.

"I don't understand how you go to Canada without any permission and—" my father ranted.

"I'm an adult, Daddy," I exhaled, stepping out of the car.

"An adult who didn't bother to book a room before leaving the country! I mean, really, Sydney? What the fu—"

I hung up on him before he could get it out. I was amazed at the entrance of The Oak Bay Beach Hotel. The lobby alone was beautiful. Wood floors that shined like diamonds, big and spacious like I was in Grand Central Station. I walked over to the reception desk on my right.

"What a beautiful day at The Oak Bay," the receptionist smiled wide at me. "Can I have your name, please?"

"Uh, Sydney Sharpe, Sharpe with an e." I watched the receptionist type away on her keyboard. "But, I haven't booked a room yet. I was hoping there would be some still available. I don't need much, really. Just a bed—"

"Sydney Sharpe? With an E?" The receptionist raised her eyebrows.

"Yes," I nodded my head.

"You already have a room. One of our penthouse suites was booked a few weeks ago." The receptionist smiled at me.

A smile spread across my face, knowing that it was J's doing. "My boyfriend must have taken care of it."

She nodded, not the least bit interested in my happiness. It took a little bit to get everything in order. When she handed my key over, I snatched it from the counter, turning around to the elevators. My heart raced, waiting for the elevator to arrive. When it chimed open, I patiently waited for a few people to step off. Once clear, I rushed in, pressing the floor of my suite.

When I left the house, I didn't have a clue if I would see J. Now that I knew he was here, in our room, and waiting for me, I could barely control my legs. I answered my father's call as the elevator went up.

"Yes?"

"Did you get a room?"

"Yep. Penthouse suite, too. I'm walking in now. I'll call you in a little," I shook my head, hanging up as the elevator chimed and the doors opened.

Walking into the suite, I was met with grand windows that housed a deck. To my left was a small bathroom with a standing shower. It wasn't impressive, but the glass doors to the bedroom on my right were nice. I walked further inside. I found a small kitchen to my left and placed my purse on the small, circular dining room table.

The living room area was a small, quaint space with a big screen TV. My mom's house was decorated better than this, but it didn't have the view the deck provided. I opened the doors to the deck, stepping on to the marble. I could see the resort in full but there were miles of water that stretched further that I could see. It was beautiful. I held onto the railing, inhaling hard and exhaling harder. The breeze blew my hair into my mouth and the scent of the water into my nostrils. This is what peace felt like.

Anxious to see J, I went back inside, calling his name out as I walked up the steps to the second level of the suite. When I made it to the top of the platform, I was in the second bedroom.

I preferred a room with the door but for the intent of this trip, I loved the open space. There was a railing that would allow me to see the body of water outside without having to leave my bed. Another big screen TV was attached to the wall in between two doors, one being a closet. The other was the master bathroom. It was bigger than the bathroom downstairs, with a standing shower, a spa tub, and double sink. It could use a facelift but outside of that, it was nice.

I was disappointed to have seen the entire Penthouse and not find J. My body ached for him. If I could just be wrapped in his arms, I'd feel better. My phone chimed with an alert.

Unlocking my phone, I saw I had one new message. It was from Ayanna. She sent me a picture of the words *I'm in love with a real life Barbie* written in the sand. Juice stood over it with his arms stretched wide. I left her message on read. It didn't stir my emotions in either direction of love or hate. I simply didn't care about it. A grand gesture would be booking me into a Penthouse Suite in another country.

Juice's guilt gifts were mild. It was always some shit I could ignore, if Ayanna would mind her business. Her little pep talks were what kept me with him for so long. The petty ass gifts were just an excuse for me to take him back. Every time Juice fucked up, Ayanna would come running for his forgiveness, sometimes before he got to apologize for it himself. It was always the same thing. She'd tell me about his childhood, loyalty, and how I needed to be his ride or die and he'd get it together for me. Well, when was he going to get it together? If he wasn't going to be the nigga I fell for, he could keep all that shit.

As I was scrolling Google, looking for a mall, or at least a store to purchase clothes from, Ayanna called me. "Hello?" I answered. I put my phone on speaker and continued my search.

"Did you see my message? I mean, I know you saw it, but you didn't say anything."

"That's because I don't care, Ayanna," I yawned, feeling tired from my flight.

"You just sliced a bitch face open over him. It sure sounds like you care."

"I care about him; I don't care about his apology. He tells me more "I'm sorry's" than he tells me the truth. I'm over it, Ayanna. Those bullshit ass gestures ain't moving me. I'm done."

I found a mall called Bay Centre and ordered a Lyft to the hotel.

"Have you even told him that? He seems to think y'all will get through. He's acting as if you're going to show up on this trip at any minute."

"Please, don't act like he hasn't already been in a bitch or two's face. I know him. He probably passed his number out on the flight. Shit. Prolly the airport," I rolled my eyes, going downstairs to get my purse.

"Sydney, please. Don't do this to him. I know he keeps fucking up, but he has no idea how much he needs a woman like you. When he sees it—"

"How long am I supposed to wait for him to see it?" I caught myself in the bathroom mirror near the front door. "I'm done proving that I'm worthy of shit that should be included in the package. Basic shit like love, affection, intimacy, respect." I walked to the elevator to get in the main lobby.

"It's just taking him a little longer. We weren't raised—"

"I'm tired of that excuse, too. Y'all had these terrible childhoods. I get it. You'd think that would make gold easily identifiable." Ayanna was frozen on the phone without a comeback. "I have to go. Have fun on your trip." I hung up as the elevator doors closed shut.

I was talking all of that hot shit, but I didn't know what

would happen when I got back home. I'd been ready to get my own place for a while. I wanted some independence from my parents, but I still wanted to be up under Juice. I could stay with my parents until I got over him and then move. Thinking about home was stressing me out. I vowed that when I stepped off the elevator, I'd spend the rest of my trip focused on finding peace. Finding J would be a plus, but it was possible that the room was a guilt gift to say he wasn't coming.

Carnage

After giving the receptionist my alias, I waited patiently for my room key. I wanted to get settled and start calling around to hotels to find where Sydney was staying. The sooner I got to her, the better — for my nerves and my heart.

"It looks like your significant other has already checked in," he smiled. "Here you are." He passed me my room key.

"Thank you."

I headed for the elevators, unable to keep my smile contained. There was a burst of warmness in the center of my chest. Sydney was already here. I didn't know how Camille hooked this shit up, but she made it happen for a nigga. My heart thumped loudly as I waited for the elevator doors to open. I wanted to run to her but kept my usual pace.

Unlocking the door and stepping in, I could smell Sydney. It wasn't her favorite perfume or a lotion she used frequently; it was her. Her pheromones hit my nose, and I got my dose. There was nothing that said someone else was staying here. Still, I was hoping to meet her in the bedroom. The top of the stairs was her bedroom, and she wasn't there. I looked behind the closed doors, still nothing. I sat at the foot of the bed.

Knowing her, she was out shopping. I pulled my phone from my pocket, stretching out with my back on the bed.

"Hey, Siri, call Camille."

"Calling Camille."

When the call started, I placed my phone on speaker and rested it on my chest.

"Did you make it?" Camille asked again, with a mouth full of food.

"Yeah. I'm in the room now."

"Then why you calling me? This could've been a text, fam. What's up?"

I hesitated. I knew what I wanted to say, but I didn't know how to say it.

"I know how you feel about me. So, for you to do all of this despite that shit, even against my will, you really down for a nigga. Thank you."

"Boy, I just wanted some dick." We both burst into laughter.

"Damn. That's how it is?" I smiled on my end of the phone.

"Nah, but forreal. It wasn't easy," she sighed. "All the things you make me feel, you already feel for her. I couldn't deny you the chance to see it through. And hey, if the shit don't work, we can just kill her ass."

Camille and I laughed again. We stayed on the phone for about two minutes more before she ended the call. Now, I was bored as fuck, stuck with my thoughts, waiting on Sydney to get back.

To keep it real, the only thing stopping me from taking it there with Camille was my father. She denied sleeping with him, but my head told me I couldn't trust it. If I couldn't trust her, I couldn't love her. Camille was tempting. She had her own flava. You could taste her energy when she walked into a room. Camille could rock any hairstyle and kill it. She was down to earth but smart as shit, and her walk turned heads. I just couldn't take it there with her.

I heard the door open and turned my head towards the steps, waiting to see her face. My dick fell in rhythm with her movement and jumped a little with each of the thirty-two steps it took to get to me. Her feet hit the platform, and the thumping stopped. All of that energy rested in the tip of my dick, almost vibrating from the intense stare we held.

"J," Sydney spoke softly, moving closer to the bed.

"What's up?" I sat up.

Sydney rushed into my lap, kissing me. One hand wrapped around the back of my neck, while the other held the side of my face like she had to touch me to know I was real. My hands held her up by her ass, and we kissed, falling backwards on the bed. I closed my eyes, wanting to increase the other senses she was touching. The small smacks of our lips sounded like music to me.

"I missed you so much." Sydney pulled her shirt off, before putting her lips to mine again.

"I missed you more." I grabbed her face with one hand and used the other to flip her on her back.

I pulled my shirt off, and she unzipped my pants. I stepped out of my jeans and pulled her panties down with her leggings. I flung them over the banister. Sydney unhooked her bra, letting it fall from her hands to the floor, next to the bed.

I bent over her body and took one of her nipples into my mouth. I let the tip of my dick play with the entrance of her pussy. She tried to reach for my dick to put it in her, but I backed up out of her reach. I kissed down her stomach, making my way to my knees. I let my lips feel on her pussy, knowing that her body was craving my tongue.

I watched her body heave up and down, anticipating a lick. When I finally got my tongue on her, her back lifted off the bed as she grabbed my head and held it in place. She used her hips to move her pussy all around my face. She came on my tongue.

I raised from the floor, picking her up and getting on the bed with her. I inserted myself in her and slid a finger to her ass. I only applied pressure as my dick went in and out of her as deep as I could get it.

"Cum in me," Sydney begged me.

There was no space between our bodies as she slid further on it and grinding, holding my hips, pulling me in.

"You want to give me a baby?" I asked.

"Mmhmm," she nodded her head. Her face frowned and her forehead wrinkled from the pleasure.

"Ahhh," I exhaled, lowly. My legs shook as I neared an orgasm. "You gonna have my baby?" I asked just as I came inside of her.

"Yes, baby," Sydney shook, cumming with me.

I laid my head against her stomach, slowly pulling myself out of her until my body laid flat. Sydney rubbed my head.

"You think the sex is so good because it's always *I miss you* sex or *I don't want you to leave* sex?"

"Nah. If we were together, in each other's faces all day, it'd be *because it's Tuesday* sex, and it'd be just as fire," I said, wrapping my arm around her thigh.

My phone rang on the dresser, and Sydney passed it to me, taking a glance at the screen first. Either she didn't think I would notice, or she didn't give fuck about me seeing. Tiana was calling. I considered letting it go to voicemail, but after seeing a little girl on my phone screen, Sydney was going to ask about it either way.

"Hey, Ma Ma," I smiled into the FaceTime.

"Hey, Daddy. Good night!"

"Good night, baby. Daddy be home in two days. Ok?" I adjusted my body to lay on my back in between Sydney's bare legs.

She passed the phone to my mother, and the romance left my body.

"Carna—" My mother showed her face on the screen.

"Yeah, Ma? I'm kind of busy." I twisted my phone to show a quick glance of Sydney's face, so she'd know that my name wasn't Carnage right now.

"Oh, I'll text you." She waved her arm before hanging up the call.

"Your mom is beautiful." Sydney tightened one of her legs around my neck.

"Thank you."

"You didn't tell me you had a daughter."

I wasn't surprised; I knew it was coming. Sydney couldn't help herself. She needed to know. She wanted the bad thoughts she had of me to be true so she could convince herself that I wasn't the one.

"I didn't. I do now. It's complicated."

"Uncomplicate it." Sydney's usually soft tone turned into one with a hint of anger.

I looked back at her, letting my face ask, *who the fuck you talking to?* She didn't budge. She was waiting for my response.

"She's not mine, but she's mine now." I gave the best answer I could without telling the full truth or a complete lie.

"I need more." Sydney ran her pointer fingers in a circle around one another. "It's not giving honesty."

I was tripping off of how much she'd changed. She had some hood in her. I wasn't sure if I liked this new her or not. It was different.

"Oh, yeah?" I raised an eyebrow, and she calmed herself.

"All I'm saying is, we have all the time in the world for you to make it make sense. Or what? Three days?" She rolled her eyes. "You giving me the weekend before you disappear on me again?"

"Nah. I'm ready now. You coming back with me."

"So, first, you try to put a baby in me, and now you want me to come home with you? It's sounding like you trying to trap me," Sydney smirked.

"It's not a trap; it's a rescue." We went silent. "You always saying you want me to save you. Here I am." I stretched my arms out.

I hadn't planned on bringing her home, but her face when she walked in, I was never leaving without her.

"What's different? Just three months ago, you were saying the opposite."

I wanted to run off with him all the other times. That was before I had a life. It was before I had something I would miss. Before Juice.

"Three months," he shrugged.

"J, I'm serious." I hit him with the pillow.

"What changed is my job. I'm basically the boss now." He grabbed the pillow I hit him with and put it under his chin.

"So, all the stuff about what I would and wouldn't be able to do doesn't matter now?" I asked.

"Nah. Yeah. I don't know. I didn't figure all of that out yet."

"You come to me with some half-assed plan, and I'm just supposed to say 'ok, let's go!'? This is my real life, J!"

"Woah. Calm down." J held his hand out.

For once, I wanted to be more than a whim. After making me wait so long, I expected a well thought out plan.

"I'm tired of picking up the pieces and creating a picture. My name is not Pamela James. I need more than that." I folded my arms into each other.

"Sydney, why are you tripping on me like this? I will figure it out. *We* will figure it out. I'm not trying to go back home without you."

"Before, that would have been enough. I *lived my life*," I used quotation marks. "Like *you* asked me to. I found a whole lot of bullshit. I need to know you, like really know you."

"We can't do that in two separate states, Sydney. This isn't some typical shit. I'm not a typical man. I don't do shit like this!"

Seeing J get upset with me gave me some type of reassurance that he was invested. Still, I wasn't letting him off the hook.

"We can't do that until *you're* ready to answer the questions you've been refusing to answer. I'll be downstairs when you're ready to talk." I got off the bed, in hopes that he would chase me, but he didn't.

Downstairs, I opened the deck doors. The breeze was too chilly to sit outside, but I wanted to feel the air against my face. I grabbed a throw out of one of the bags I'd brought in earlier. I wrapped it around my body and sat in front of the deck, doors wide, watching the waves.

Juice would never let me walk away from him. Kyle either. It felt dumb comparing them, but those were the only examples of romantic love I'd had. I wanted to believe they loved me but made mistakes. Maybe they never did, and those weren't mistakes and it was them acting from their core selves.

"You hungry?" My pussy kegeled at the sound of his voice.

I nodded my head, not bothering to turn around. I was starving. My last semi real meal was at the airport. I grabbed a pastry while shopping, but it did nothing to fill me.

After J ordered us steaks with mashed potatoes and string beans, he sat down behind me, giving me a good squeeze.

"I'm ready to talk. Whatever you want to know." He kissed my shoulder. I wished I didn't have the throw over me so I could feel his lips against my skin.

"Let's start with your real name. What does J stand for?"

"Jerard. My given name is Jerard Essex. I prefer to go by Carnage."

A coldness blew across the back of my neck despite the throw around my shoulders. My body turned on against my will.

"Carnage?" I asked softly with wonder.

"Yes," he whispered into my ear, and my body shuttered as he gave my earlobe a gentle nibble.

"Why Carnage?" I leaned back, eyes closed.

"I'd tell you, but I'm scared you'll run from me." He planted another kiss on my shoulder as he removed my throw.

The cold breeze mixed with the warmth of his breath made my body shiver.

"I could only ever run to you," I said, barely above a whisper.

The silence was loud. I was getting horny anticipating the truth.

"Why Carnage?" I asked again.

"Because I kill people." He moved my hair behind my ear and kissed the nape of my neck. "You ok with that?"

I nodded my head. I instantly felt protected and wanted to give him all of me. I panted as his hands moved to my pussy. I wanted him.

"Room service!" Hotel staff was knocking at the door.

I whined.

"Relax. I'm not going nowhere." Carnage got up to get our food.

I forgot how hungry I was until the food took over my nostrils. I jumped up to get to my plate. Carnage sat at the small dining room table while I ate at the kitchen counter, unable to wait any longer to eat.

I tried to look away from him as he ate, but I couldn't. My brain wouldn't stop trying to picture him killing someone. I couldn't see it.

"Mostly with a gun. I prefer to use my hands, but it's not often I get the chance because most kills call for discretion." Carnage stuck a fry in his mouth like he was telling me about the weather.

"Huh?"

"I'm good at reading the room. You want to know how I kill people."

"So, it's your job?" I cut into my steak.

Carnage only nodded his head.

"And you're the boss now? So, if you didn't want to kill anyone anymore, you wouldn't have to?" I picked his brain.

"Technically, you're right."

"What do you mean *technically*?"

"I mean, if I wanted to stop, at this point, I could. But, I don't want to. I mean, I tried. But it keeps me sane. Levelheaded."

"Most people smoke weed for that. Have a drink or two after work," I shrugged.

"Most people aren't me. I don't know how to explain it but —"

"What does it feel like?" I joined him at the table.

"What does *what* feel like?"

"Taking someone's life. Do you feel like God?"

"I don't know what God feels like. It gives me a dose of power. I feel powerful, limitless, alive. That last breath is like a hit of crack. I'm assuming because I've never done it."

That was a relief. If he was doing those type of drugs, that would seal the deal. Yet, he tells me he murders people, and I was still there with him.

"You scared of me?" he asked.

"Should I be?"

"Not unless you the FEDS."

"Did you kill Jemma?" I blurted out.

"If I tell you—"

"You'd have to kill me?" I twisted my lips. "How original."

"Marry me." Carnage stared at me.

I searched his face for a sign that he was joking. Nothing. I must've heard him wrong.

"What?"

"If I tell you, you'd have to marry me." He stood from his seat, making his way over to me. I was stuck. "For the record, I'd never kill you. It would make me feel powerless." He kissed me. "Limited." He planted another kiss. "Dead."

The last peck turned into a full-blown kiss. Next thing I knew, I was naked in the kitchen. I made love to a murderer, and I liked it.

"Hello?" I answered the hotel phone.

"Good morning, Mr. Essex. This is your 7 a.m. wake up call. Please be ready to depart for your adventure by 9 a.m. Thank you."

"Wait, I'm sorry. Adventure?" I cleared my throat.

"You have a full itinerary for today. Your assistant requested a wakeup call for today and tomorrow."

Camille was always doing some extra shit. "I don't know if I have the energy for two days of adventures, but thank you."

"Oh, tomorrow is not a day of adventure, just one event."

"Well, what is it?" I was curious.

"I'm not at liberty to say. Enjoy your day, sir." The receptionist ended the call.

"What's going on?" Sydney yawned, cuddling against my chest.

I would've rather stayed in the room with her all day. I didn't need to go anywhere.

"Apparently, my assistant has a day planned for us."

"Oh, is she responsible for booking this room? I thought I'd have to find one and was prepared to get scraps, but this was already in my name."

"Yeah, she takes care of everything for me. I wasn't going to show. Daughter woke me up, saying we had to go," I gave a small laugh.

"Why weren't you going to show?" she asked me.

"You never hit my phone. I thought you was over it. Figured you moved on."

"If I'm being honest, I was seeing someone. I almost didn't get on the plane to you. Some bullshit happened, and I said fuck it."

"I figured. We gotta get ready, though." I sat up, and her body moved off of me.

I moved around the room, gathering my things for a shower. After fucking last night, we dragged our asses upstairs, and got straight in the bed.

"Are you mad?" Sydney asked.

"Nah. Why would I be?"

"Oh," Sydney said.

She went into the bathroom. I heard the door lock. I thought it was weird that she took the time to make sure I didn't come in.

By the time she stepped out the shower, I was laying the last of my things out. Watching her in just that towel made it hard for me to keep my hands to myself. We'd laid around long enough and had to go.

She went downstairs and came back up with hella bags she grabbed when she went shopping. She pulled out a few outfits, holding them up to her body, trying to figure out which to wear.

"I like the yellow," I told her, walking into the bathroom for my shower.

The water felt good hitting my skin, but I rushed my

shower to make sure we got out the door on time.

I stepped into the bedroom to see Sydney chose the green outfit instead. It didn't matter what she had on. She would turn heads regardless. She led the way downstairs to the lobby, and I noticed she hadn't said anything since we talked about the nigga she was dealing with. While we waited for the shuttle, I grabbed the back of her shirt into a knot and pulled her into me.

"Shuttle's here." She walked away, and I followed.

The shuttle took us to Butchart Gardens. It was one of the greatest gardens in the world. I didn't give a fuck about no flowers. I'd been here before. Sydney looked to be enjoying the tour, but I was too focused on her energy. Something was off.

"What's wrong with you?" I asked, taking a sip of water, trying to read her body language.

"Nothing," she rolled her eyes.

"Oh, you're one of them?" I raised my eyebrows. "Got it," I nodded my head, closing the cap to my water bottle.

"One of who?" Sydney's fists balled, and her feet stood in perfect stance to get a good jab to my face.

"One of those women who'd rather say nothing is wrong, when really, something is wrong, but by the time you're ready to talk about it, everything is wrong."

Sydney exhaled, trying not to smile. "I'm upset that you don't seem to care that I have a boyfriend." She started walking again. "Makes me think you must have a girlfriend." She cut her eyes at me.

"To be clear, you *had* a boyfriend. I'm your boyfriend now." I gave her a straight face, so she knew I was serious 'bout that shit.

"That's what I meant," she looked down, grabbing my

hand.

"And I don't care nothing 'bout that nigga." Sydney nodded her head. "The only real girlfriend I've ever had is you." I watched her blush.

Sydney wanted to grab as many pictures as she could. I faked excitement when she did. We walked around the garden for two more hours before boarding the shuttle again.

We arrived at Victoria Butterfly Garden, and Sydney was excited. She grabbed my hand, rushing me off the shuttle to get inside.

"You've been here, too?" she asked, walking in.

I nodded my head. "Sorry," I shrugged. "No reason you can't enjoy yourself, though."

"It's not the same if you've seen everything already." Her hands hung at her sides.

"I'm just happy to be with you, I'm good." I kissed her temple, pulling her close to me as we walked.

The butterfly garden was more like a rain forest. Exotic birds flew around. There were bodies of water with turtles, poison dart frogs, and koi. She ain't do too much until she saw the flamingos. That put the biggest smile on her face.

After the garden, we grabbed dinner from Blues Bayou Café. Sydney ordered some Voodoo Dippin' Cauldron, which was basically spinach dip but better, a half Bayou salad that I had several bites of. I ordered a large gumbo that she thought was hers. I was willing to bet money she had more of my soup than I did.

Southern Comfort Loin of Lamb was her entrée, while I had Blackened Voodoo Top Sirloin with sautéed mushrooms and roasted garlic and a double order of shrimp. We spent about two hundred including the tip and the three drinks Sydney had. We left there, full.

Back at the suite, I laid across the couch with Sydney on top of me, gazing out at the water. She looked at the tattoo on my forearm, tracing it with her index finger.

"Did any of your tattoos hurt?" she asked.

"Pain is pleasure. You feel them, but they don't technically hurt. If anything, you want more."

"I've always wanted one, but my mother never stops reminding me that they're permanent."

"They are. I know tattoos are more of a trendy thing to do, but all of my tattoos mean something to me. I thought about each one carefully before tatting it on my body."

"What about this one? Why a wolf?"

"What does a wolf represent for you?" I asked her, seeing if she could figure it out on her own.

"They usually run in packs, but there's also the lone wolf saying. I'm not sure," she shrugged.

"Protection of my family. Strength, loyalty, courage, and hunting. It means a couple of things. It's on my forearm because my family gets on my fucking nerves sometimes. I need to remind myself that I'm a part of a pack and to behave as a wolf would."

"What about this one?" She pointed to the Lily with the words, *Breathe for her*.

"That's for my grandmother. Her name was Lily, but lilies represent gratitude. It's on my stomach because that's my core. That's where I'm fed. She taught me a lot of shit that I'll carry with me forever. Knowledge I want to pass down to my kids."

"I never met any of my grandparents. Well, I don't remember meeting them because they all passed by the time I was three. I wish I had something to carry on from them."

"You want kids?" I asked her. I was ready to commit my life to her and didn't know much about her ass.

"I don't know. Some days, I wake up and I'm grateful that I don't have any. Other days, I wake up and I'm ready to be nine months pregnant," she laughed.

"How do you feel about being a stepmom?"

"I'm scared as shit," Sydney laughed nervously. "I think I'd be a great mom, but what if she doesn't like me? When do I speak up? When do I mind my business? Is any of it my business? It's a lot, but I'm ready."

It was easy to say you were ready, but I wasn't all the way sure that either of us were. It was going to be a big adjustment for everyone. First off, Shany has never liked any woman she thinks I'm even a little bit interested in. I was used to having my own space; even Tiana being there was a lot on me. I needed to decompress after a job. Only silence would get me back right. Sydney was moving to Maryland without the comfort of her parents. My fear was that she was ready in the moment but when it came down to it, she had no idea what she was getting herself into. Neither did I. We'd have to take it day by day and figure it out together.

You think a Penthouse Suite sounds like the shit until hotel staff is knocking at the door, and you have to walk down a flight of stairs to answer.

"I'll get it." Carnage walked past me.

Since I was already down the steps, I plopped down on the couch. I had to see who was at our door.

"My nigga!" A man stood, arms stretched open.

"What's good, fam?" Carnage pulled dude in a for a hug.

The other guy was pushed inside when a woman came storming in behind him. "I need you out of here." She spoke to Carnage and pointed at the door.

She turned to me. "You're Sydney? I didn't imagine you to be this damn pretty. I'm Camille, his assistant." She pointed to Carnage. "Can you stand up for me?" She grabbed my hands, pulling me up from the couch. She forced me into a spin.

I was annoyed. As his assistant, she should be playing the background. Instead, she was moving around the penthouse as if she'd paid for it. I was aware that she'd booked it, but I assumed the money came from my man's account. I made eye contact with Carnage, and he read my mind.

"Uh, Sydney, this is my homeboy, Geppetto. It's cool to call him G." Carnage walked over with his hand on G's shoulder.

"Nice to meet you. I've heard a lot about you." G held his

hand out to me.

His energy felt better than that Camille bitch, who was moving around in our bedroom now. I met his hand with mine, and he lifted it to place a kiss to the back of my hand.

"Aye, nigga. Cut the shit," Carnage eyed him.

"Nice to meet you, too," I smiled as Carnage wrapped me under his arm.

"Y'all ready for today?" G asked with a wide smile.

"Huh?" Carnage asked.

"You're not about to ruin my surprise." Camille finally exited our bedroom and walked down the steps. You had one job, Geppetto. Take Carnage the fuck outta here."

"For what?" Carnage put his hand on the back of his head, stretching his neck, frustrated.

"Get him out of here, please." Camille began to shoo them out of the suite. I was leaning on the edge of the couch, watching Camille watch the guys walk down the hall. "I'll be right back," she said before disappearing herself.

I couldn't get a read on her, outside of the fact that she did too fucking much. Carnage said that he was the boss, but it seemed like she was. It was hard for me to imagine a woman being around him and not wanting to submit to him immediately. I was slightly intimidated by the power she had over my man. She said jump, and I was surprised he didn't ask how high.

When she returned, I was in the same spot with my arms folded into one another. She burst through the door with a wide smile.

"Welcome to the family." She held the door open.

A woman walked in with a suitcase rolling behind her and

a curling iron in the other. My hair was in knotless braids, so I wasn't sure what she planned to do with that. Another woman entered behind her with a similar suitcase but deep purple and carrying an LED gel nail polish lamp. The last woman walked in with a slew of dresses on a rack.

"What's all this?" I used my hand to point to the last girl.

"You're getting married!" she beamed.

A hot flash took over, forcing me to pace the room. I'd always planned to be a wife, but I wasn't ready. I was supposed to be learning how to love myself all over again. Carnage had just begun opening up to me. I still had so much to learn about him. My stomach felt heavy. Time slowed down. My eyes darted around the room like I had a hit of a heavy drug. Every small sound that would normally go unnoticed was as loud as my panic.

"Everybody get out!" I yelled, hands moving up and down.

"What's wro—" Camille tried to speak to me.

"I just need a second to think! Alone! Please," I begged, not knowing what I would do if she refused because I had no energy to fight.

"Ok," Camille nodded her head. She did a come-hither motion, and the other three woman followed her out of the suite.

I ran into the bathroom and splashed water on my face. If I was dreaming, this was the time to wake up. My reflection in the mirror was as overwhelmed as I felt. My phone rang, and I jumped, hitting my head into the mirror. I rubbed my head, going on a search for my phone. The ringing was coming from the bedroom. I took my time up the steps.

I rushed over to my phone when I saw the name *J* and made a mental note to change his name in my phone.

"Hello?" I sat on the bed, staring out at the water.

"Sydney, I am so sorry. I don't know what Camille was thinking. She's always doing the most."

"You don't want to marry me?" I asked. I wasn't sure if I wanted to marry me, but hearing that he wasn't interested, stung.

"No, I did. I do," he exhaled. He was as overwhelmed as I was. "The original plan was to ask you to be my wife this weekend."

"You want me to be your wife?" My smile couldn't be contained. My chest drummed as warmth took over my body. I went from panic to a calmness I'd only felt with Carnage.

"Yeah. I do. But we don't have to do this today, Sydney."

Everything leading up to this moment flashed through my head. All those emotions came and went, with my thoughts always circling back to him. He made me feel good. I wanted to feel like that every day for the rest of my life.

"I want to marry you," I spoke softly with my mind made up.

"Sydney, this is serious shit. My world... it's—" he paused. "You might not like it there."

"Will you be there?" I asked, getting off the bed and walking down the steps slowly.

"Whenever you need me." Carnage was easy going. "I'm not worried about us making it. I know we will. I'm concerned that you're being forced into doing something you don't want to do. We can do it somewhere down the line. I only want you to be comfortable."

"If you're there, I'll love it there. Let's do it." I laughed into the phone, unable to hide my excitement.

"I guess we're getting married then. I love you."

"I love you, too." I ended the call.

I stared at my phone in disbelief before swinging the suite door open to find Camille. She and the three girls were standing there.

"Took you long enough. Let's go!" she clapped her hands. "We lost an entire twenty minutes. Get moving."

"Did you pick a dress yet?"

"No." I rushed over to her, going to each dress until I found the one that made my heart beat out of my chest. "This one." I held the dress up.

"Well, put it on." We don't have much time." She checked her watch.

I ran upstairs, excited to get my dress on. I'd imagined this day would be me surrounded by my mother and bridesmaids helping me prepare. Doing it alone felt intimate. When I saw the way it fit, butterflies filled my stomach.

"It fits. Right?!" Camille yelled up the stairs.

"It's perfect!" I called out. "How'd you know my size?" I started making my way down the steps.

"Geppetto is an animal with that tech shit. He went through your credit card purchases and found your size for me."

"My credit card purchases?" I asked, walking down the steps. "Does he kill people, too?" I whispered to Camille.

"We do not have time to get into everyone's dirty laundry. You look fucking amazing." Camille smiled wide at me.

"I feel it," I smiled shyly.

"Let's get hair and makeup settled."

I felt like a princess being waited on hand and foot. Camille had an off-putting personality, but she met my every need. She insisted that I was as much of her responsibility as Carnage was. It was showing in the catering she was doing to me, but I still wasn't a fan.

After about an hour and a half, we were done. I stood in front of a full-length mirror, wanting to cry. I didn't because I didn't know any of these bitches, but I thanked them profusely. I couldn't wait for Carnage to see me.

I was walked downstairs where Carnage was standing in the lobby, waiting for me.

"You look good as shit," Carnage licked his lips.

I chose a long sleeve mermaid dress with a V cut. Lace was all over to just below my ass, and everything that followed was ruffled. It was colored the softest pink that the unknowing eye would think was white.

"Thank you. You look better than me," I laughed.

Carnage was dressed in a white tuxedo. The jacket was a honeycomb print and set the entire thing off. The one diamond in his ear shined as bright as the sun. He had a fresh shape up. I couldn't wait to get my hands on him.

"Lies." He kissed me.

A white Cadillac Escalade pulled up. Pushy ass Camille rushed us outside.

"Get in. We'll see you shortly." She literally pushed us both into the truck and slammed the door behind us.

"She always like that?" I asked him.

"Unfortunately, yes," he nodded. "She's good people, though," he shrugged.

It was burning my chest not to ask if he'd fucked her. Today was not the day, but the day would come.

We were dropped off to a grass field. The only thing there was a helicopter. Carnage got out of the truck and reached for my hand. I looked at his hand like he was crazy. I leaned forward to speak with the driver.

"Is there any way you could drive us to wherever this helicopter is supposed to take us?" I asked.

"Yes, ma'am. I could get you there in about forty-five minutes."

"That works for me." I leaned back in my seat.

"Sydney!" Carnage yelled at me.

"But there's a hike once you get there. You don't seem dressed for that activity." He smiled through the rearview mirror.

"See," Carnage raised his eyebrows. "Come on." He held his hand out again.

"I don't do helicopters," I shook my head, as we walked over, hand in hand.

"Look at it this way, if it goes down, at least we go down together," he smiled.

"You are not Romeo, and I am not Juliet. There is nothing romantic about dying together," I rolled my eyes, climbing into the helicopter. Carnage climbed in behind me.

The ride was only about eight minutes, but it felt like an eternity. My heart beat through my chest. I squeezed his hand like I was in labor. A puddle had formed between our palms. I didn't give a fuck; I wasn't letting him go.

We were dropped off at the top of a mountain. The view from our balcony had nothing on the view here. I could see everything. The wind blew over us, and warmth overwhelmed me, causing tears to flood from my eyes. Looking at Carnage and this view, nothing else mattered. I had everything. My parents could enjoy the pictures. The moment was for me anyway. It was for my memories — not theirs.

G and Camille stood off to the side as the officiant began to speak. I tuned him out. Carnage and I stared into each other's eyes. We communicated without words. I could hear him saying he loved me, and I repeated it back to him, hoping he heard me as clear as I could hear him. It wasn't until my name was called that I snapped back into the moment.

We went with the basic vows and said *I do* where necessary. When Carnage placed the ring on my finger, my tears flooded my face. It was me. Beautiful and expensive. If I were a ring, this is what I would look like.

When the officiant said we could kiss, I tongued him down. I wanted to fuck him right there on the top of the mountain. He promised we could come back one day and make it happen. If I didn't know anything else about Carnage, I knew he was a nigga of his word.

We had a two-hour photo session. Most of the poses were at the top of the mountain, but there were a few along the hiker's trail. I think my favorite was the one taken with the drone hovering over us as we stared into the other's eyes.

After photos, we had a small cake waiting for us. I was completely against cutting into it, wanting to save its entirety for the freezer. Carnage, Camille, and G forced me. I cut into it but refused to remove the slice. They got their little picture, and I got to keep my cake.

The helicopter took us back where we were dropped off, and a limo waited for us. Inside, was a tassel diamond party dress. Carnage and I talked as I changed.

"This is *not* how I imagined my wedding as a little girl," I laughed. "But today has been nothing short of breathtaking."

It was truth. The only thing that could've made it better was having my parents there. I had to erase them from my thoughts because whenever it crossed my mind that I had to tell them, I got sick to my stomach. My father had always joked about how we were going to be the flyest father and daughter to walk down the aisle. And my mother might have a heart attack. This was my moment; I didn't want to be consumed with what they would think.

"I didn't think I'd be a husband."

Carnage hadn't stopped smiling. I wanted tears when I walked down the aisle. I didn't get them, but this smile was childlike and had the same effect. The smile etched on his face was how I felt on the inside. It felt good knowing that for once, the love was mutual.

Carnage

The limo took us to Bar None Nightclub. The dress Sydney changed into had me ready to say fuck this club and go back to the room. It was important that Sydney have her night. I mean, it was my night, too. It meant something to me, but I'd prefer if it were just the two of us. We'd gone so long apart. We'd spent more time with other people than we had alone. I was ready for that part. The part where it was just the three of us—Sydney, Tiana, and me.

I talked shit but inside the club, I turned up with my wife. Everything about the night felt right. I was a whole husband in these streets. My smile was holding strong. I felt good.

Camille had the DJ announce that we were married. We didn't spend any money because the club goers purchased us drinks all night. Syd danced up on me, making my dick grow in the middle of the club. The last song of the night, Sydney and I were tongue tied on the dance floor.

I carried her midair, both hands on her ass, to the limo. I laid her down on the back seat before getting in myself and shutting the door.

I instructed her to hold on to the back seat headrest and arch her back. I kissed from the top of her crack to the tip of her pearl. She controlled my dick with her whimpers. I kissed my way back up before Sydney reached around and forced my face to bury in her ass. She flexed while my tongue went in and out of her ass, ending with a suck that led to me slurping her juices from her pussy. She trembled, cumming into my mouth.

After the second orgasm, she begged me to stop, but I only switched holes with each orgasm for the forty-five-minute ride to the suite.

Back at the hotel room, Sydney was on go. She walked through the Penthouse door, coming out of her clothes. Her dress and undergarments were left like breadcrumbs up the steps.

"I want to get fucked from the back, looking at the water." Sydney held onto the railing, poking her ass out.

My dick was hard, but I took my time getting up the steps, making her wait for me. I took my time undressing. She whined for me, and it made me harder. I grabbed her scarf from the pillow on the bed and tied it around her eyes. I pulled the belt from her robe and used it to tie one of her hands. I used the belt from my jeans to tie the other. She stood there, naked and trembling.

I held my dick at her entrance, only allowing it to apply pressure without inserting it inside of her. I ran my free hand across her spine, barely touching her and watched her body shiver. She begged me to put it in her. Still, I held back until she begged, calling my name.

Women only knew J. I'd never heard Carnage called out, and the shit sent me. I slid inside of her slowly. She exhaled as if her thirst had been quenched. She relaxed, allowing me to work my way into her deeper. My calves tightened with every stroke forward, as I tried not to cum before her. I'd made her cum repeatedly in the back of the limo, but that wasn't enough. Those were oral orgasms; she needed to cum from penetration to feel fulfilled.

She tightened around me. I pulled out of her, on the verge of cumming and rested my head on her back. The more she whined for me to go back in, the more I held back. I kissed down her spine, trying to give her what I could until I was able to give her what she wanted.

"You tapping out on me?" she moaned.

That shit hit my ego, and I went back in her on a mission. I stroked into her, hitting her cervix. The fact that she liked it and wanted more, made me go harder and faster until the both of us were cumming. My God, I loved her ass. I could do this shit for the rest of my life.

"Untie me, please." All of the sexy left Sydney's body as she fell to the floor. Her hands were still in the air, and her head rested on one of the poles to the banister. She'd looked like one of my torture victims. I used the little energy I had to untie her. Neither of us made it to the bed. We fell asleep, dick to ass, right there on the floor.

∞ ∞ ∞

I woke up to Sydney admiring her ring. Her hand was on her heart, and her eyes twinkled. I saw her wipe a tear that fell and let her know I was up.

"Good morning, wife," I kissed her shoulder, pulling her tighter.

"Good morning." She turned her head slightly to kiss me.

"How long you been up for?"

"Not long. I was just about to wake you up," she smiled. "I know your assistant planned our wedding, but you picked my ring, right?"

"I did. How can you tell?"

"Because this is a ring for a worthy woman. I'm not talking about the price. Like, the cut of the ring, the way it sits perfectly on my finger. You saw this ring and thought of me." I nodded my head because everything she was saying was truth. "I've never been with a man who knew my worth. I love it here." Sydney kissed me with her morning breath.

We had a slow love making session where she rode me while begging me to cum in her, and I did. She fell onto me just as my alarm went off.

"It's time for us to get out of here," I rubbed her back, placing a kiss to her forehead.

"I'm not ready." She clung to me.

"You don't have to go back home if you don't want to say goodbye to your family. If you don't have anything you'd like to have at home with you, you can get on the plane with me to Maryland."

Sydney was quiet, in deep thought.

"I guess I do have some things I need to wrap up back home," she twisted her lips, lifting off of me.

"Don't take too long, though."

"Two or three days should be enough time," Sydney said, as I packed my things.

"And wrap shit up with that nigga you were with. Let him know what it is and leave him there. I don't want to see that nigga calling your phone. I need that shit dead before you get on the plane, including the new attitude you have."

"Ok," Sydney said, softly.

I knew she was going to go see the nigga. Women thought they needed closure. I wanted her to know she wasn't sneaking to do it. But after this goodbye, I didn't want to hear shit about that nigga again.

"Shit, I don't have any luggage for my things," she bit her lip.

"There's space in mine. I'll take it home for you."

"Home, huh?" she smirked, walking over to me.

"Aye, get in the shower. You get to touching me, and we'll never get out of here." I pointed her to the bathroom.

After her shower, I jumped in. I knew she had to give her farewells, but I wanted her on the plane with me. I'd spent too many days without her, and the thought of not seeing her face for two or three had my head fucked up.

We left the suite together and rode together to the airport. When we separated for our gates, Sydney had tears in her eyes, having to leave me. I thought of missing my flight so that I was leaving after her, but I missed Tiana. I needed to get home to my baby.

"Before you go, did you kill Jemma?" she whispered in my ear, immediately pulling back so she could see my face."

I nodded my head.

"Why?"

"I'll tell you when you get home."

"I'll be there soon." She gave me one last kiss.

She nodded and I boarded the plane. I wasn't sure what that confession would do for our marriage. It was possible she'd never make it home to me. If that was the case, then it just wasn't meant to be. I took my mind off my worries and switched my focus to my family. They were going to kill me when they found out I got married.

Sydney

I was anxious the entire flight. Every part of me wanted to be on the plane that Carnage left on. I took my ring off as I headed out of the airport. It still hadn't settled that I was a wife. It was going to have to settle quick because I was in my father's car, headed home. I told my parents that I needed to talk to them both tonight. Against my father's will, he was heading inside the house with me.

"Before we go in here, you're not pregnant again, are you?"

"No, daddy. I'm not pregnant," I rolled my eyes, getting out of the car.

"I'm just asking!" He shut his door, following me with his arms up.

"Please stop yelling outside of my house like that. This is not the hood." My mother opened the door for us.

"Can I have a hug before you start yelling at my father?" I asked, giving her a hug and kiss in the cheek.

"I'm sorry, honey. How was your trip?" She rubbed my arms up and down.

"It was cool," I shrugged.

"You complain if I'm not interested. You complain if I'm interested. I don't know what you want from me, Sydney." She threw her arms up.

"She wants you to act like a real adult for once. You

prancing your little boyfriend around here. Now she has to watch how she's dressed in *her* house." My father took a seat at the dining room table.

"Nigga, get out of my chair. I didn't offer you a seat. You can stand. Whatever Sydney has to say is not going to take that long. Come on." My mother made the come-hither motion. "Out my chair."

"Your new man got you talking like that? I don't think I've ever heard you say *nigga* correctly," my father laughed, playing with a toothpick in his mouth.

He got me doing a lot of things you ain't never seen," my mother spat, sitting down.

I tried several times to interrupt them, and they weren't listening. After five more minutes of them going back and forth, I interrupted.

"I'm married!" I screamed, sliding my ring back on my finger.

"Excuse me?" My mother's neck snapped viciously.

"I'm married," I swallowed hard.

"So, when you said you were taking a vacation, you were really eloping," my mother nodded her head. "Got it. I am really trying, but you are testing my patience. I lighten up and *this* is what you do?"

"It wasn't planned. Well, we didn't plan it." I defended both me and Carnage.

"Who is we? I mean, really Sydney, who have you been dating long enough to marry?" My mother was laughing. It was scaring me, honestly. I expected tears of pain, not anger.

"Let me see this boy." My father held his hand out for my phone.

"What does that matter?" My mother sucked her teeth, holding her hands to her head.

I scrolled to a picture of us and slid my phone across the table to him. I folded my arms into one another. I watched my father nod to himself.

"So, how do you plan to be married, living between your mother's place and mine?"

"I *know* you're not okay with this." My mother's mouth hung open.

"I trust my daughter to make good decisions. She had a year of learning some hard lessons."

"That's exactly why I don't trust her decisions. She's sneaking around like a child, and you think she's ready to be married? Make it make sense."

I wasn't understanding my father's calmness either. It was clear he knew Carnage. I was curious as to how.

"I'm moving to Maryland," I confessed.

I thought they'd be more upset about me eloping and led with that.

"I've been considering going back to Maryland," my mother said, not missing a beat.

"No, Mommy!" I stood, pushing my chair backwards. "I'm doing this by myself. I don't need you there to hold my hand."

"Fine. When is all of this supposed to happen?" My mother rubbed her temples with closed eyes.

"Two days. I only came home to tell you both my plans and to pack my things," I played with my ring, avoiding eye contact.

"Two days?!" my mother yelled.

"Pack your things, and I'll ship it to you," my father said.

"Are you kidding me?" Her neck twisted as she spoke to my father.

"The girl is going to do what she wants. She's already proven that." My father directed his open hands towards me. "I'd rather my daughter be comfortable wherever she is, and I'd like an address, in case I need to go running to her."

"Good. I'm glad y'all have this shit figured out because when this marriage blows up in her face, she can call you," my mother stormed off, wiping her eyes.

I was fine until she said that. My lips trembled as tears broke free and fell to my cheeks.

"Aww, baby girl." My father got up, pulling me into his chest. "She doesn't mean any of that. She's scared for herself as much as she's scared for you. She doesn't know who to be without you. She'll be fine." I nodded my head.

It was long before my father left. I didn't have the energy to pack a thing tonight. I went to bed with the plan of packing in the morning.

∞ ∞ ∞

The next morning, my phone rang. I smiled as if I hadn't been dead tired and in need of more sleep. One of our wedding pics covered the screen with the word *Husband*.

"Good morning," I answered, anxious to hear his voice.

"Good morning. Why didn't you hit me before you went to sleep?"

I talked to Carnage while waiting for the flight attendants to let us off the plane and promised I would call before bed to let him know how things went with my parents.

"Last night was a lot. I got in bed and passed out. I'm sorry."

"It didn't go well?"

"My father handled it well. I was prepared for my mother to turn on the water works, and she did. Only, she was angry, not sad. I feel bad."

"You can stay if you want."

"Not that bad," I laughed.

We talked for another twenty minutes before I heard his daughter in the background. She was hungry, so he said he had to go. She sounded sweet and innocent, but most kids did. Then, they terrorized you in private.

I opened my door to use the bathroom and moving boxes fell over. My father said he'd bring some by in the morning, and he kept his promise. My mother bringing them in let me know that she was still upset, but she was okay. She could've left them outside — or worse — thrown them away. I hoped she came around before I left for Maryland. I'd hate for us to be on bad terms while I was so far away. It wouldn't be easy to repair with so much distance between us.

After washing my face and brushing my teeth, I went back into my room. I packed only the things I couldn't live without. My phone rang with Juice's name and face. He called me several times while in Vancouver but after Ayanna's call, I put my phone on DND. The few texts he'd sent, I left on read. I was surprised he was still calling. I took an exhale before answering.

"Hello?"

"What's up?" Juice's voice was low.

"Hey." I stopped packing to focus on our conversation.

"This weekend wasn't the same without you," he confessed after a few moments of silence.

"Yeah? I wonder how that could've been avoided." Men never started with the apology. It was always a warmup of sweet nothings to see if you were receptive or not.

"I'm sorry, Barbie. I know I keep fucking up, but I'm done, I swear. I will never hurt you again."

"Thank you for the apology, but we need to talk."

"I can come get you or you can—"

"Tomorrow. I'll come to your place."

"Okay. I can't wait to see you."

"See you," I said before ending the call.

Carnage giving me the green light to see Juice was a relief. I knew I was going to see him, and guilt hit my chest at just the thought. Carnage being understanding was all the more reason for me to hurry up and get my ass to Maryland to my man. Tomorrow, I'd go talk to Juice and have him drop me off at the airport, if he wasn't the emotional asshole he tended to be when things didn't go his way.

I moved around my room, continuing to pack when my mom knocked on my door.

"Can we talk?" she asked, stepping into my room and closing the door behind her.

"Yeah."

It'd been a while since she barged in before I gave her permission to enter. Considering her emotions being all over the place, I let it go. I was happy she came to talk to me. I wasn't sure what would happen if I left before we made up.

"I am not happy about you running off and getting married."

"But momm—"

"*But* you are a grown woman. I have to respect your decisions. I hope you've been through enough heartache to know one hundred percent that this is the man you want to spend the rest of your life with. Marriage is not easy. Living with a man is not easy. And being away from both of your parents is not easy. I'm sorry for the mean things I said yesterday. I'm just so scared for you. But If I'm being honest, I'm more scared for myself."

I nodded my head, trying not to smile. As much as she and my dad argued, he knew her well. She'd die if she knew he predicted her ailment before she did.

"I've made a lot of progress in this *unsmothering* process." She used air quotes. "Therapy has not prepared me for my daughter, my only child, moving to another state on her own to a man I don't know. Still, that is my issue, not yours. I need you to promise me one thing."

"Anything." I regretted it as soon as the words left my mouth.

One thing with my mother could be the hugest ask. I got too excited about us making up and spoke too fast. My heart raced, fearing the worst.

"If at any moment, you feel like you want to come home, call me." I nodded my head as my eyes watered. She grabbed hold of my arms. "Forget what I said last night. I don't ever want you to feel like you have to struggle with any amount of pain to prove me wrong. You can *always* come home." She pulled me into a tight hug.

The guilt lifted from my shoulders. Pulling away from the hug, we were both wiping our tears while laughing at how emotional we were. She helped me tape and stack the rest of my things. We sipped wine while talking about our fondest memories together.

When my head hit the pillow for the night, I called Carnage.

"What's up?" He answered the phone.

"Did I wake you? You sound like you were asleep."

"I dozed off. It's been a long day."

"For me, too. I finished packing, though. My dad is going to send my things and my car once I get there."

"Sounds good." Carnage was half sleep.

"Go ahead to sleep. I'll see you tomorrow."

"See you tomorrow. I love you."

"I love you, too." I hung up with a smile on my face.

I was so anxious to get home to him, I wasn't interested in seeing Juice anymore. I thought about changing my phone number and blocking him on social media, but a man would always find a way to contact you. It was best that I ended things completely before I left.

$$\infty \infty \infty$$

The original plan was for me to say goodbye to my parents, say goodbye to Juice, and have him drop me off at the airport. My parents weren't having it. They wanted to see me off at the airport. They argued about whose car I would ride in. I made the decision that we'd all ride in my father's car. I chose him because I knew no matter how upset my mother made him, he wouldn't leave her on the side of the road. I wasn't sure the same applied for my mother.

I told them I needed to make one stop, and my father obliged. I saw Juice step on his porch and got out of the car. I took a mere four steps before turning back around to take my ring off.

He was already going to be hurt. I didn't want to crush him.

"Hey," I said, standing at the bottom of the steps.

"What's up?" He walked down the steps to meet me. "You look nice."

"Thanks." I gave a small smile.

"Look, I'm sorry. I know I be doing stupid shit," he shook his head. "I feel like I'm not good enough for you. I'm constantly moving around, feeling like you're going to find somebody better. So, I did all that dumb shit to protect myself when you did. I'm off that, though. I'm gon' act right from now on. I promise. I dead ass love you, Sydney."

"You would've been enough. You were enough before you went and fucked all those other bitches. I forgive you, but I can't do this anymore. Thank you for the apology. I deserved it, but it's too late." My lips trembled.

I watched him raise his arm and clench a handful of his dreads. He bit his lips, trying to contain his emotion, and all of mine came spilling out of me. I stood there, arms folded, crying, refusing to face him anymore. I looked down the street while I talked through the burning sensation in my throat.

"I'm moving back to Maryland."

"That's what's up," Juice spoke slowly.

"Take care of yourself." I finally looked to him, wiping my eyes.

"You, too," he nodded, looking up at the sky. "Be safe."

"Thanks." I walked away with my hands in the back pockets of my jeans.

"Aye, Barbie." Juice called out as my hand touched the handle of the door. I looked back at him. He stood with both hands in his pockets, fidgeting around. "I love you," he confessed.

I nodded my head, gave him a smile, and got in the car. My father pulled off after hearing my seatbelt click. I took my ring from the cup holder and placed it back on my finger.

It was a silent ride to the airport. I wasn't sure if they both knew I wasn't in the mood, or if they were trying to deal with their own emotions. It was heavy, but every part of me wanted to be with Carnage. I knew I was making the best decision for myself.

Outside of the airport doors, my father stood with his hands on his hips, while my mother tried to find something to do with her hands.

"The second I get your mother home, I'll have your things shipped out." My father nodded his head. "You have any trouble, you call me, okay?"

"I will." My father pulled me in for a hug.

My father had freed me all of two seconds when my mother grabbed me, pulling me into a hug.

"I'm going to miss you so much, baby." We rocked back and forth.

"I'm going to miss you, too."

My mother placed a hard kiss to my cheek, before my father placed one to my forehead. Neither of them wanted me to leave. I grabbed my Nike bag from the ground and slowly walked backwards. If I didn't take control, the two of them would make me miss my flight.

"Now, why you think you getting your ass in my backseat? I'm not your damn chauffeur, woman," my father spat at my mother, grabbing the handle to the back door.

"I rode in the backseat over here, and that's how I'm riding home." My mother scrunched her face.

"That's because my daughter was in the front, where she belongs. Now, you gon' get ya ass in that front seat, or you'll be riding with Uber."

"You get on my motherfucking nerves, Elijah, you know that?"

I laughed, walking fully into the airport. They'd be out there arguing for hours. Now that all of my goodbyes were out of the way, I only had the future to look forward to. I couldn't wait to get to Carnage and start our lives together.

Carnage

"Daddy, I don't want to go to school no more." Tiana had her arms folded across her chest with her lip poked out.

She was sitting on my lap while I was tying her shoes for her.

"Stop tying her shoes. I showed her how. I don't want her relying on anybody."

"She's *my* daughter." I twisted my neck towards Shany.

"And *my* niece. She needs to be independent. How she supposed to do that when you keep doing everything for her?"

I ignored Shany and focused my attention back on Tiana. "Why not? You not making any friends, Ma Ma?" I played with her three poof balls of hair. She had one at the top and two at the bottom.

"They mean to me."

"Stop crying. Anybody be mean to you today, you push them on the ground, you hear me?" Shany instructed.

"Why are you telling her shit like that?" I added bass to my voice, and Tiana started crying harder.

"What are y'all in here doing to my granddaughter?" My mother walked out of the bedroom in a Nike sweatsuit and her purse on her arm. "Let's go, Tiana."

She climbed off my lap, running to my mother and hugging her leg.

"Give your father a kiss, so we can get on out of here." Tiana came over, poking her lips out, and I turned my cheek for her to land it.

"Thank you, Ma Ma." I kissed her forehead. "Have a good day, okay?"

"Okay," she pouted.

I waited for them to pull out of the driveway before getting up from my seat and stretching. "I'm about to get out of here."

"I don't know why you keep coming over here every morning anyway. It's a waste of time and gas." Shany put a bagel into the toaster.

"'Cause, I want to see my daughter off to school." I walked into the kitchen with her.

My mother was doing better, but only with Tiana present. If I tried to take her home, she'd be a crying mess. It was frustrating. I took Tiana to school on her first day. My mother rode in the back seat with her. Josie suggested that I allow our mother to take Tiana to school as a way for her to get out of the house. Otherwise, she'd be in her room all day. I agreed, but I wanted these moments, too.

"You need to pick Tiana up and just take her home," Shany shrugged.

"No! He can't do that. Tiana is the only thing holding mommy together." Josie walked into the kitchen.

"Maybe that's what she needs, Josie. To fall apart for a second. She has an unhealthy attachment to Tiana, and it's doing more harm than good. To her *and* Tiana."

I was ignoring my sisters' arguing until Shany said that.

I didn't know what was wrong with my mother, so I didn't know how else to fix it, other than letting her have Tiana when she wanted. It wasn't clear if she was fucked up because she killed my father, or if she was fucked up about finding out who he was. Any attempt at clarification on which it was, she'd shut down. She didn't want to have any conversations about my father. Something was going to have to give soon because I wanted Tiana home with me and Sydney.

"Tiana will be fine," Josie rolled her eyes.

"Will she? She's going to be as codependent as mommy if Carnage doesn't take her little ass home. Mommy is a grown woman. She gon' have to figure this shit out," Shany shrugged, pulling her bagel from the toaster oven.

"Of course, you think that. Daddy made you hyper independent, and it's fuck everybody and everything. You always come first to you!" Josie yelled, eyes watering.

Shany was unmoved, spreading cream cheese across her bagel. "Maybe if you had a little more independence, you'd stop creeping from closet to closet with that little bitch and live in your truth."

Josie's mouth fell open. She stormed out of the house and slammed the front door.

"Why you do that?" I shook my head at Shany.

"Do what? Tell the truth?" Shany twisted her lips. "We already know the girl is gay. Mommy doesn't acknowledge it for whatever reason, so she keeps tiptoeing in and out of here. If she'd just move with some damn confidence, mommy will just have to deal, but the both of you so worried that she's going to break," she rolled her eyes, biting into the smaller side of the bagel.

"What I got to do with this?" I put my hand to my chest.

"You do it, too. Mommy is not a weak ass bitch; she pretends to be because y'all let her. Leave her to fix herself, and she'll get herself together. Soothing herself with your daughter ain't helping nobody. Mommy's getting worse, Tiana is too dependent, you not happy because you want your daughter home. I love my niece dearly, but I don't even remember the last time I got some dick."

I looked at her, frowning.

"What?" she shrugged.

I grabbed the bigger side of her bagel and made my way to the front door.

"What the fuck, Carnage?!" She threw a butter knife at me.

"It's for my pain and suffering." I bit into the bagel, getting into my truck.

I'd been anxious all morning, preparing to pick Sydney up from the airport. My normal routine was going to change drastically, and the worst part was that I hadn't told my mom or my sisters yet. They were going to flip the fuck out. I'd deal with them later; I didn't want to taint my excitement about having Sydney with me.

A glance at the clock made me speed. It was close to eight a.m. I wanted to make sure everything was perfect when Sydney arrived. My place was always neat for the most part, but I hired a maid for the day, just to make sure I didn't miss anything. She was set to arrive at eight and leave by two.

She finished at eleven, but I paid her for the rest of the time. I passed out, watching *The Equalizer* on the couch.

My alarm woke me up when it was time to pick Tiana up from school. If it wasn't for Camille, none of my alarms would be set. I knew my mother was picking her up, so I took my time in the shower. After grabbing Tiana from my mom, I was going straight to the airport to grab Sydney. I wanted to look and smell my best for her.

When I got to my mom's, she was already waiting with the water works.

"Hi, daddy!" Tiana took her little apron from her neck and ran over to me.

"You here to pick Tiana up?" my mother pouted.

"Yes, ma'am." I scooped Tiana up in my arms. I planted a kiss on her cheek.

"I'm not ready, Carnage. Can she just stay for a little bit longer? I just need a few days."

My mother's eyes were sad, but that wasn't why I agreed to let Tiana stay with her. Sydney and I could use some time getting familiar with our new lives, just the two of us. My daughter was safe with my mother and my sisters. I'd pick her up Sunday morning and introduce everyone to Sydney at the same time. I left my mother's and headed for the airport.

It didn't take long for me to notice Sydney in the crowd of people. She stood out like a diamond amongst dirt. She sauntered over to me, both hands in her hoodie with an infectious smile on her face. I was forced to smile. I stood with my hands in my pocket, watching my wife walk over to me. She stood on her tiptoes, giving me a kiss. Her hands went around my neck, my hands wrapped around her waist. I forced us apart, knowing we could get lost in our kisses and fuck right at the airport doors.

"How was your flight?" I grabbed her Nike bag from her shoulder.

"It was cool. I was anxious the entire flight."

"Why anxious?" I opened the passenger door for her.

"Mmm," she shrugged. "I left everything familiar for the unfamiliar. I'm just hoping Maryland is good to me."

"If it isn't, we can go." I pulled into traffic.

"You forreal?"

"I am."

She grabbed hold of my hand, getting comfortable in her seat. "I hope we're going to get food because I am starving."

"We can."

I took Sydney to Moe's Seafood. She was so impressed by the food; she took two orders of other food she wanted to tryhome to eat later. I tried to convince her to have one of their fire ass drinks, but she insisted on laying off the alcohol. We'd been on the road for twenty-five minutes, with close to an hour drive left. I could see Sydney falling asleep and turned my music down for her. I always wanted her to be comfortable.

"Why did you kill Jemma?" Sydney asked, staring at the night sky.

She wasted no time finding out the answers to what she wanted to know. I expected a little prying but not a full dive in like this.

"Because I was paid to," I answered.

"By who?" Sydney leaned forward.

"Someone who wanted her dead."

"But who would want her dead?" Sydney leaned back in her seat, thinking.

"Judge Decker." I didn't have to tell her anything, but I was interested in her reaction.

Her mouth dropped, and she leaned forward again.

"Jemma was pregnant. By him," I revealed.

"Bruh, it really be real shit going on behind the scenes," she shook her head.

"When I told you to leave that nigga in Florida, I meant everything you got from him. Stop talking like that."

Sydney leaned back in her seat, crossed her arms across her chest, and poked her cheek with her tongue. I didn't give a fuck about how she felt about it. My girl didn't talk like that. The rest of the ride home she sat quietly. I hummed along to the radio, and it was getting under her skin. Shit was funny to me.

When we parked, I got out of the car and opened her door for her. She reluctantly took my hand, stepping out with me. I wrapped her under my arm as we walked into the apartment building. She grabbed my arm, interlocking her fingers with mine. I put a kiss on her forehead as I opened the door. We walked over to the elevators.

"Fancy."

"I thought that was a requirement for you."

"Shut up." She slapped my chest.

We got on and off the elevator in all of sixty seconds. I led the way to the condo. I was as nervous as she was. Camille had me second guessing myself by insisting that I get an interior designer before Sydney arrived.

I put the key in the door as we walked in. "Whenever you're ready, you can go shopping and replace every piece of furniture except my bed. My California King stays." I pointed my finger at her while shutting our door. Sydney stood at the entrance, looking around. I couldn't get a read on what she was thinking or feeling.

"Damn, it's that bad?" I put my keys on the end table before taking a seat on the couch.

"No," she laughed. "You mind if I look at the rest of the house?"

"I guess I should be giving you a tour," I stood up, walking her around. "First, you don't have to ask. This is every bit of your place as it is mine."

"I don't want any claims to this condo you've shared with your hoes," Sydney rolled her eyes.

"I don't bring women to my home."

"And Camille?"

"What about her?"

"Does she come here?"

"Yeah. She's my assistant," I shrugged, not seeing what the big deal was.

"But you haven't fucked her?"

"Never."

"I find that hard to believe. If you haven't fucked her, she wants to. I can feel it whenever she's around."

"I don't think that's the case. Either way, I am a happily married black man. And black men don't cheat," I kissed her, opening Tiana's bedroom door. "This is Tiana's room."

"That's your daughter's name? Tiana?" Sydney gave a small smile, looking around at her room.

"Yep. I call her Ma Ma most of the time." I shut her bedroom door before moving on to the bathroom.

"Is there a master bathroom?" Sydney asked, walking around the guest bathroom.

"Yeah, fancy," I laughed, leaning my back on one side of the door and stretching my arm to the other.

"I'm asking because this bathroom is fancy as fuck. I'm excited to see what the master bathroom looks like," she laughed, leaving the bathroom. She touched the knob to my bedroom door, glancing back at me. I nodded my head for her to open. "Oh, my God." She walked in.

"What?" I was slightly offended.

"Really? A King bed and a big screen TV? That's it? You have all this space, and you're not using it right," Sydney shook her head, walking into the master bathroom.

"California King," I corrected her.

"Boring ass King." She looked at the toilet seat. "Imma need you to get that together." She pulled the seat down.

I laughed. "I'll work on it." I wasn't used to putting the seat down.

This bathroom is nice, though. I can't wait to light some candles, fill the tub with hot water and bubbles, and sink into the water," she inhaled, looking like she was climaxing from the thought alone.

I pulled out my phone, sending Camille a text to bring candles fitting for a bath. Females were mad particular bout their candles, so I wanted to be specific.

"You can take one tonight," I moved around her. I plugged the tub, turned the knob for the water and grabbed some of Tiana's bubbles. "I hope these will do until we get you some of your own," I laughed, getting off my knees.

"If this is what I have to look forward to, I can't wait to get to forever," Sydney kissed me.

"We already here." I put the lid down and sat.

I pulled her leggings down, then her panties, helping her step out of both. I pulled her shirt over her head, taking her bra off. She stood in front of me naked, and my dick jumped in awe of her shape.

I turned the water off, seeing the tub was full and helped her step in.

"Thank you," she smiled at me, resting the back of her neck against the tub.

"Oh shit, my bad." Camille stepped into the bathroom.

"What the fuck?!" Sydney grabbed the curtain, pulling it back to cover herself.

"I was just bringing the candles." She stepped just outside of the bathroom.

"Why you ain't knock?" I ran my hands down my face.

"I did! You didn't answer, so I used my key," she shrugged.

"Key?!" Sydney peeled from behind the curtain, grilling at me.

"Thank you." I grabbed the bag of candles from her.

"You're welcome. I'll see myself out." Camille walked out.

I pulled the candles from the bag, setting them out around the bathroom. Once Sydney heard the front door slam, she moved the curtain back.

"Why is she slamming doors like somebody did something to her? And why the fuck does she have a key when I don't have one? I live here, right?"

Sydney ran off question after question. I was starting to sweat. I'd never been in this predicament and gave a fuck. Camille and I were going to have to set boundaries because Sydney was with none of the shits.

I assumed that the first night in my new home, I'd be passed out on the floor somewhere from being fucked out of my body. That shit was dead the second I heard Camille's voice. For her to just walk in like that, and then for Carnage to act like it was no big deal, I was blown. He said it was handled but considering she was on her way to the house again, it didn't feel like it.

"Ugh!!!" I yelled, frustrated with opening cabinet after cabinet and not finding coffee or tea.

All Carnage had was water and Gatorade. I didn't want that right now. To deal with Camille this early in the morning, I was going to need an extra boost.

"What's wrong?" Carnage ran his hand down his face.

"Can you have your assistant bring some coffee since she's on her way already?" I rolled my eyes.

"Yep." Carnage pulled his phone from his pocket and hit a few buttons. "Anything else?" he asked.

I was prepared to argue. Even in all of my anger last night, Carnage refused to argue. If it was something he could fix, he just fixed it. I stared at him, stalling, until I could think of something else I wanted.

"Yeah. I need a key. Preferably the one Camille has."

Carnage twisted his lips. "That'll get your attitude together?"

"Mmhmm," I smirked. "What exactly is she coming here

for anyway?"

"So y'all can go pick out furniture and shit."

"I don't need her for that."

"And I don't need your attitude, but I'm getting it, ain't I?" He looked at me. "I think y'all could use the time together. I've already spoken to Camille about boundaries that need to be set moving forward."

"Good," I mumbled.

"*In the meantime,*" he bassed on me. "You will need to build some kind of rapport with her. She's still my assistant. I need you to be comfortable with her."

"You can't get a new assistant?" I asked, straight faced.

"Not in my line of work. I have to trust everyone around me. I don't trust easily. It would take me a long time to find someone as skilled and as trustworthy as her. Is that a problem for you?"

I wanted so bad to try my hand, but I could feel it in the air that he wasn't going for it. I had to get a little something extra in, though.

"If I get her key, I can deal."

Carnage shook his head, walking out of the kitchen. "Fine."

I followed him into the living room, and the front door opened.

"Oops. My bad. I forgot," Camille smiled.

She stepped behind the door, shutting it and knocking on the door.

"You talked to her about boundaries?" I twisted my neck at Carnage.

"Come in!" he yelled to the door, not bothering to

acknowledge what I'd said.

"I am so sorry, I'm just so—" Camille started to speak, and he cut her off.

"It's cool." Carnage rubbed the back of his neck. "But, I'm going to need your key back. Sydney needs—"

"I can go get her one. That's no problem. You like those little cute ones from the display, or you want a plain key?" Camille looked to me.

I was considering letting her make me a key because I did enjoy the little designs. It's not like I'd spend much time looking at it, but it was a part of my extraness. I didn't want the same dirty gold key that everyone else used for their homes.

"I need that one." Carnage pointed to the key ring Camille held tightly to in her hand.

Camille's mouth dropped open. It took everything in me not to smile. My man sided with me. I planned to suck the skin off his dick later as a thank you. She grilled Carnage as she took the key from its ring. Her eyes never left his.

"I should throw this shit at your head." She stepped forward to hand him the key.

"Now, why would you do that? I'm trying to keep the peace. When the two of you get acquainted, we can talk about it but until then, it is what it is," Carnage shrugged.

"I take it, this is for you as well?" She looked at me, lifting the bag with coffee pods.

"Thank you." I took the bag from her hands, ignoring her glare.

She wasn't the first bitch to look at me crazy, and she wouldn't be the last. If it came down to it, I'd pour my coffee down her fucking throat. I walked into the kitchen to make my coffee. I tried to be as silent as I could so I could listen to any words they exchanged. They were silent. I began brewing my coffee when I heard the front door open and shut. I stepped out of the kitchen, taking a peek into the living room.

"Looks like it's just you and me." Camille smirked at me.

"Fun," I said sarcastically.

"I'm not sure if it was miscommunicated, but I'm not a fan of yours either. I thought I'd be able to look past this bougie bullshit, but it's looking like that ain't going to happen. Unfortunately, I still have a job to do. So, where do you want to look for shit at?"

This bitch had done more than rub me the wrong way. Carnage had never done anything to harm me, but finding myself in a new state with my murderous husband was scary. I didn't think he'd kill me, but I wasn't interested in seeing what he would do if I didn't at least try to get along with this bitch. I let out a deep exhale before throwing a small body temper.

"I was thinking At Home, Home Goods, and Ashley's furniture. Those should do. I'm open to any suggestions as I'm sure you're more familiar with the area than I am." I grabbed my mug when my coffee finished brewing.

"Good choices. I'm ready when you are."

"I just need a second." I walked off into our bedroom to slide into my flops.

When I packed my small carry on to get me through until my things arrived, I hadn't packed a single pair of sneakers. It was mostly warm in Florida, even when it rained. I hadn't accounted for Maryland weather and wasn't properly prepared. I felt a breeze when Carnage slid in from the balcony door earlier and knew I'd be freezing. I had too much pride to ask Camille for shit else. I already felt like I was apart of the remedial class, having Camille assist me to begin with.

"That's what you're wearing?" She scrunched her face up at me.

"Are you a fashion designer too?" I rolled my eyes. "Let's go."

"Girl! It's cold as shit outside, but if you want to freeze, that's fine with me," Camille laughed, walking out of the apartment, laughing at me.

I'd freeze before I asked this bitch for anything else. I was going to speak to Carnage about asking for anything on my behalf moving forward. If he couldn't do what I needed, I'd figure that shit out for myself.

In the car, Camille stopped at Panera Bread. She got an orange juice and some kind of toasted sandwich. I only got a bowl of fruit. She whipped left and right hard, making the car swerve, all the while holding her sandwich with one hand. She'd taken two calls, avoided a deer, and escaped every red light. She was a great multitasker. All I got from that was that she could handle being my husband's assistant and sucking his dick.

Ashley's furniture was our first stop. I wanted a brand new living room set. There was no telling how much pussy Carnage had gotten on that couch. I promised him I wouldn't go too girly, but I was absolutely going to get rid of it if he was allowing me to.

I chose a chocolate sectional with attached recliners at both ends, and a chocolate love seat with a matching ottoman. I was going for a teal and chocolate living room. None of it would be delivered until the weekend. At the register, Camille swiped my husband's card. I sent Carnage a text that I needed my own card. The bitch acted as if she was doing me a favor to spend my man's money on me. If anything, she was the fucking help.

Ayanna called me while we were in Home Goods. To be honest, I'd expected her to call the second I left Juice's porch.

I pointed at my phone before walking a few aisles away from Camille.

"Hello?" I answered.

"What's up?" Ayanna sounded dry. She wasn't calling to see how I was doing; she was calling to see why I hadn't called her.

"Shopping for my new place. What's going on with you?"

I held some photo frames up to get an idea of what they'd look like around the house. We didn't have enough pictures to go hanging shit on the walls, but it was a goal. Having the photo frames would be motivators for my vision.

"Shit. Wondering why my *best* friend hasn't said a word to me about moving? I mean, fucking really, Sydney?! You leave and take the time to say goodbye to Juice's ass but not me? Who was wiping your tears when he made you cry? Me!"

"Actually, I wiped them myself. You were too busy trying to get me to stop crying long enough to forgive Juice," I rolled my eyes, picking up random things in the next aisle.

I wasn't the least bit concerned with Ayanna's attitude. So, I didn't tell her I was leaving. Who gave a fuck. It wasn't as if I had all day for goodbyes.

"If that's how you feel."

"I mean, I don't really feel any way. That's you. I haven't called because honestly, I don't want to hear shit about Juice. You can never leave him out of our conversations."

I was becoming annoyed. I was dealing with enough, being forced to deal with Camille. Ayanna was laying the guilt trip on thick. It wasn't working.

"So, we don't have our own relationship outside of him?"

"I thought we did, but that's all you talk about, Ayanna. I don't want to talk about him. I'm married and—"

"Married?!" Ayanna's voice screeched.

I immediately shut my eyes. It wasn't necessarily a secret, but I wasn't trying to share that with her yet. She was going to run it right back to Juice and like I said, I didn't want to crush him. I just didn't want to love him.

"Yes. Married."

"That's why you moved. It all makes sense now. So, what the fuck was Juice? A placeholder?"

I stopped in the aisle, and my mouth fell open. There was no way I heard her correctly.

"Yes. He was a placeholder for the nigga ready to give me it all. I was his fucking doormat, so I guess we're even. The next time you call, leave his name out of the conversation. I'm a fucking wife now. Have some respect. Or you can not call at all." I ended the call.

I exited the aisle to see Camille standing there. She didn't try to pretend she wasn't listening.

"Trying to keep old friends with a change of lifestyle *this* big is damn near impossible. I don't have a single childhood friend." Camille gave me a soft smile, and we walked down the next aisle together. "I still have a male friend or two, but friendships with men are easily maintained." She slurped her smoothie. "Women, on the other hand, they want all the details. There're not many details you can give when you're in this business. They never understood. Slowly but surely, those relationships dwindle. I wouldn't stress it."

Carnage and I needed to talk. I wanted to understand how his business worked. Camille made it sound bigger than what he did. I wanted to hear, from his mouth, what I'd gotten myself into. Plus, I was just plain old nosey. He never told me how he was in charge now. I wanted to know everything. When we finished shopping, I had Camille swing me by the grocery store to grab a few things to make Carnage dinner. She offered to drop me home and do the grocery shopping alone from a list, but I didn't want her to think I needed her. I didn't. Carnage did. If I had any say, he wouldn't need her for much longer.

Carnage

The sun shined exceptionally bright, or maybe I was closer than usual. I sat parked in a rental in downtown Baltimore. I was hunting. I hadn't done any heavy jobs.

One, because I didn't have to anymore. I'd been waiting for the moment I could keep my hands clean. My trigger finger wasn't in agreement. It'd been itching to kill something.

Two, Sydney wasn't ready for me to be gone for days at a time. The mental preparation of becoming someone else before leaving, the isolation while gone, and then the decompression I needed to get back to myself would be too much for her. So, I was keeping it local and taking any small jobs I was sent.

I needed shit that didn't require me to get close to the target. Nothing where I had to learn my victim. To make shit easier for me, Camille found random local stories online. She'd send me screenshots or video links of anything she felt was deserving of death. If I agreed, I made them a target. Quicks kills, requiring no clean up.

This job was to take out a Baltimore City bus driver by the name of Suzanne Rochester, an older black woman, who was set to retire this week. In a Facebook comment that Camille sent, dude said his mom got into it with Suzanne. For months, she skipped her bus stop on purpose. Once his mom was late to work so much, she was fired. Lost her apartment, then her car. She was on the street, begging for money at one point. Ultimately, it ended with her being raped and killed, landing him to be raised by his grandmother. That was death worthy in my opinion.

I studied her face for a week, and this was the first time I had a chance to get away from Sydney.

Every time the MTA building door opened, I was on alert. When I saw a balloon, I knew it was her. It made sense; there'd be a retirement party for her departure. My smile was as wide as hers as I started my engine, following her.

I ended up in Owings Mills. She lived in a neighborhood with trees and a perfectly manicured lawn. The second her engine cut off, I grabbed my gun. She opened the door, holding tight to her balloons so they wouldn't fly away. I sped down her street, landing one shot through her passenger side window. In my rearview mirror, I watched her balloons fly away and her body fall from the car. I stopped at the stop sign like I would any other day, before pulling out of sight.

That kill did what it was supposed to do. It'd hold me over for a few. If it just got me through the marriage announcement with my mother and sisters, I'd be grateful.

I stopped by the apartments for a quick shower. Oneisha was standing in the center of the living room, braiding some girl's hair.

"What's up?" I mumbled as I walked past her, not interested in any conversation.

Oneisha rolled her eyes, but the girl in the chair got excited. "Heyyyy." I heard her mumble, "who the fuck is that?" before I opened the hallway closet. My clothes were on the top shelf.

"Girl, a big fucking nobody!" she said, making sure I heard.

"Shit. He look like that nigga to me."

"Shut the fuck up," Nesha tapped her.

I took a glance at the girl in the chair. "I'm married, sweetheart, but thank you." I blew her a kiss before shutting myself in the bathroom.

"You a fucking clown!" Nesha yelled out.

I didn't give a fuck about her attitude. I bet you it was fucking spotless in this bitch. She knew not to play with me like that again. She could suck her teeth until they fell out her mouth, but she knew I'd kill her ass whenever I felt like it. I didn't want to see much more of her ass and was considering getting another spot, tucked off somewhere. I could have Camille check on Nesha and be done with her ass.

After my shower, I shot over to my mother's crib. They were all in the living room when I walked in the door. It was my first time seeing my mother chilling outside of her bedroom in a while. That was a good sign. My news might send her back to her room.

"Daddy!" Tiana came running to me.

I scooped her up as she jumped in my arms. "Daddy missed you, Ma Ma." I kissed her cheeks while tickling her.

"You taking me home?" She wrapped her littler arms around my neck.

"Yep. You ready?" I asked her.

"Mhmm," she nodded her head.

She reached for my hand, and it was all over. "Daddy, I want a ring, too." Tiana got excited. My mother and sisters all turned their heads at my hand at the same time.

"We'll get you one, okay?" I was talking to Tiana but looking at my mother.

"What you wearing that for?" Shany was the first to ask.

I cleared my throat. "Because I'm married." I was still focusing on my mother. I searched her face for any change that said things were going to get worse.

"Excuse me?" Josie laughed.

"I got married." I took a seat in my father's recliner.

"No, you didn't," Josie laughed, looking around the room. "There's gotta be a camera somewhere. This has to be a joke."

"Or a check. You marry one of them foreigners for some money, baby?" My mother and Josie fell out together, laughing at my expense.

"I don't think any of this shit is funny," Shany stood up. "Mommy say something to him." Shany held her hand out in my direction.

"What do you want me to say, Shany?" My mother sucked her teeth. "He's a grown man. What do you want me to do? Monitor his dick?"

"Mommy!" Josie yelled.

"Chill on me." I twisted my neck at all of them.

"The rest of y'all running niggas and bitches in and out of here. Your brother deserves love, too." My mother looked directly at Josie.

"You knew?" Josie's eyes watered.

"Before you did," my mother smiled, grabbing Josie's chin lightly.

"Can we focus on the issue?" Shany punched her fist into her hand.

"All I know is, this wife of yours better have her ass here soon, so I can meet her." My mother pointed in my face.

"She can't come here," Shany twisted her lips.

"My *wife* can go wherever I go. I know it's unexpected, but I'm trying to do it the right way. I could've just walked in the door with her. Do whatever you need to do to get over it," I shrugged. "Come on, Ma Ma."

"Bye," Tiana waved to everyone.

"I'm not playing, Carnage," Shany called out.

"Neither am I," I said, shutting the door.

I put Tiana in her carseat before taking off for home. During our drive, I prepared her as best I could.

"Daddy's friend is at home. She's going to be living with us, okay?" I took a peek through the rearview mirror to get her reaction. I went with *friend* because wife was complicated. I could explain that to her later.

"Is she nice?" She dug in her Ziploc bag of snacks.

"She's really nice," I assured her.

"What's her name?"

"Sydney."

"Ok, but she can't sleep in my room."

"She's going to sleep in Daddy's room." I took another peek.

"Like mommy used to?"

It'd been weeks since Tiana mentioned her mother at all. I hoped she had forgotten about her, but clearly, she hadn't.

"Yeah, Ma Ma."

"Is Sydney my new mommy?" Tiana asked.

I thought this would be a quick conversation, but it was turning out to be an interrogation. I didn't know how to answer these questions.

"How about this, if you like Sydney and want her to be your new Mommy, she can be. It's up to you, okay?"

"Okay," Tiana giggled. "Can Auntie Shany be my new mommy? She not mean no more. I like her."

"I'm glad you like her now, but she can't be your mommy. She's your auntie, ok?"

"Ok." Tiana pouted a little.

Tiana dozed off for the rest of the fifteen-minute ride. I tried to get her out of the car and in the house without waking her, but her head popped up as I turned my key in the lock.

"You can go back to sleep," I whispered, opening the door.

"I want to meet Sydney." She wiped her eyes of the crust that formed during her nap. She looked wildly around the room.

"Hey, baby." Sydney stepped into the living room and popped her robe open to show her naked body. "Shit." She ran back into the kitchen.

It was too late. Tiana was giggling from seeing Sydney naked. "Daddy, put me down." She wiggled until I set her feet to the floor. She made it to the kitchen before me.

"Hi, I'm Tiana. I like your robe." I walked into the kitchen to see Tiana waving.

"Thank you. I like your shirt." Sydney bent down, using her Megan knees. "My name is Sydney. Tiana is such a pretty name. A pretty name for a pretty girl." Sydney tickled her a little.

"Thank you," Tiana blushed and left the kitchen.

"It smells good in here. I could smell the curry from the hallway." I pulled Sydney up, giving her a peck to her lips.

"Why didn't you tell me you were bringing her home?" Sydney said tight lipped, smacking my chest.

"Why didn't you tell me you were naked?" I smirked.

"It was a surprise. I thought we were picking her up together, so I could meet your mom and your sisters." She stirred the pot.

"I need a few days for that."

"Why?" Sydney pouted.

"My sister wants to fight you," I laughed. "I'm going to give her a few days to calm down."

"Well, I know how to fight now, and I don't fight fair, so she can try."

"She will," I laughed. The shit was funny, but I knew Shany would really try it. It didn't matter what Sydney had learned, she wasn't fucking with Shany.

When dinner was ready, we sat in the living room as a family, while I watched the news. I wanted to catch the story of my kill on the bus driver. I was focused but could hear Sydney and Tiana talking in the background. It all sounded like mumbles because I was zoned into the news reporters. My kill was the last story of the night.

"A Baltimore City bus driver was killed the day of her retirement celebration. Baltimore City Police say they received a call early this afternoon from a couple that a woman was laid out beside her car, bleeding. Upon arrival, they were unable to find a pulse and pronounced her dead on the scene. Mrs. Rosetta Alexander worked for the MTA for forty years, and residents remember her as being generous. Several members of the community say she'd often give them bus fare when they were short. If you have any information, please reach out—"

"Daddy!"

"Yeah, Ma Ma, what's up?" I focused my attention on Tiana.

"I'm sleepy."

"Yeah? Let's get you in the tub and in the bed."

I dealt with bath time while Sydney cleaned the kitchen. I was grateful they did her hair because washing her hair had been a struggle for me. I stood her up in the tub, wrapping her hooded unicorn towel around her. I carried her wet tail to the bedroom, standing her on her bed as I dried her off and rubbed her down with lotion. I allowed her to put on her own pajamas. It took longer than necessary, but she had to learn. After tucking her in, I kissed her good night before leaving her room.

"Daddy, I didn't say good night to Sydney." She popped her head up from the bed.

"I'll go get her for you," I laughed to myself.

I went to Sydney in the living room to tell her Tiana wanted to say good night before I took a seat on my recliner. Their first meeting couldn't have gone better. I'd been worried about everyone adjusting to my new life with a wife, and the only one who seemed concerned was Shany.

Sydney came back into the living room, sitting on my lap.

"When you were uber focused on the news, Tiana asked me if I knew her mom and if I knew where she was." Sydney lifted her eyebrows.

"What'd you say?" I asked, cutting the TV off.

"The truth. I didn't know. I know you know what happened to her mother."

"I killed her," I confessed.

The second we were officially married, the truth flowed freely. It was a weight off my shoulders not having to walk around with these secrets. Even if Sydney didn't like it, I still felt good about being able to tell the truth for once in my life.

"Why?"

I gave her the long story of what happened and why. Everything led back to my father. He wasn't a conversation I wanted to have. I'd like to forget the nigga existed. Sydney pried, and I didn't have a choice but to answer her.

"But you didn't kill your father?"

"Nah."

"How do you feel about him being gone? I mean, I would've been upset, but I'm not sure I'd be okay with someone that close to me dying."

"It's like he died twice. The man I read about in that journal wasn't the man I knew. My father wasn't the person I thought he was. I grieved for two weeks before he died. Then, when he died, I felt relief and pain all at once. I don't know how to describe it, honestly. I had to make sure Josie was straight, then my mother."

"What about Shany?"

"She was straight, to be real. She trusts me. She's probably going through it on the inside, but I don't think it's nothing she can't work through. Josie either. My father taught us the black and white of things. No grey areas, so I guess we all see he had to go," I shrugged. "My mother took it the hardest. When I went by today, she was better. She normally has a fit when I try and take Tiana, but she handed her over today and demanded that I bring you to meet her." I squeezed Sydney's back.

"But how do *you* feel?"

'I'm cool. It is what it is. I'm doing what I need to manage my emotions."

"Killing people?" Sydney asked.

I nodded my head, looking into her eyes.

"Can I get some of those emotions?" Sydney lifted gently, sliding me inside of her.

Being inside of Sydney was like a massage. I could fall asleep in her pussy. She fucked with her soul. I could feel every piece of her. I couldn't wait to put a baby in her.

It'd been a week since I met Tiana. She was a joy. All the personality in the world was in that little body. She was legit a funny ass kid. I rode with Carnage in the mornings to drop her off at school and then in the afternoons to pick her back up.

This morning, Carnage said he had business to take care of. So, I dropped Tiana off by myself. Drop off went well, but I was obsessing about what he was doing.

A lot could be blamed on my own insecurities. I jumped straight into a marriage after two heartbreaks. Well, I wasn't sure if Juice broke my heart, but the shit hurt, for sure. I was struggling with thinking Carnage was cheating or off killing someone.

Whenever he came home, I looked for signs of either and got nothing. I didn't know him well enough to get a read on him without him being direct. Often, I wondered if he was purposely blocking me from feeling his energy. He answered all my questions, and it always sounded like the truth, but I couldn't help but feel that he was still holding back. On top of all of that, I often felt lonely.

Outside of the drop offs and pickups, I was in the house. Carnage was home most of the time, but I still felt alone. I was becoming homesick. I missed my parents, my routine, my things. My things hadn't arrived yet, but the furniture had come. Decorating gave me something to do. After decorating, this place felt more like home, but something was missing. It felt like I'd invaded his and Tiana's privacy despite how welcoming they were.

I still hadn't met his family, and it was bothering me. He may have been able to survive being isolated, but I wanted to be in the mix. It felt like he was hiding me. It'd only been a week, so I was trying to keep my worries at bay, but whenever I was left alone, the negative thoughts took over.

I pulled up to the school to pick Tiana up and found someone's raggedy son pulling on her coat. I left the car running, jumped out, and ran to her. I yanked his hands from her, pushing him gently, but he still fell over.

"Tiana, you ok?" I looked all around her body. The last thing I needed was Carnage thinking that I abused his child the first time I was left alone with her.

"Brent, why are you on the ground?" A short thick, dark-skinned woman walked over to the little boy I'd just pushed.

"That lady pushed me." He pointed towards me.

"Excuse me?" his mother asked, looking at me like I was crazy.

"He was yanking on my daughter. Teach your son to keep his hands to himself." I threw my hair behind my back, walking away. "Come on, Tiana." I grabbed her hand.

"I tell you what, the next time you put your hand on mine —"

I turned around, hitting her in her mouth. I grabbed the wet floor sign and hit her over the head with it. She only stumbled. The other parents grabbed their children up, while teachers screamed for someone to call the police. I realized I fucked up. I scooped Tiana up and rushed inside of the car. I plopped her in her car seat.

"Buckle up." I shut the door, running around to the driver's side and getting in.

I pulled into traffic like I robbed a bank. After driving for a few without hearing police sirens, I calmed down. I peeked at Tiana from the rearview to see if she was okay. She was drinking out of her sippy cup without a care in the world. That was a relief. If I had scared her, it'd be a big dent in our relationship.

"I'm sorry I hit the lady in front of you," I told her. "I was just angry that her son was picking on you."

"Daddy said it's okay to hit people when they hit you first. But Auntie Shany says don't let nobody talk to me crazy." She took another sip.

"They're both right. How was school?" I asked her, trying to change the subject. I didn't want to be the one influencing her in any way. I wasn't her parent.

"I had fun. I drew you something." Her tiny arms tried to reach her book bag that was on the floor of the car.

"You can show me when we get home, okay?"

"Ok. I'm hungry."

"Me, too. Let's get some pizza!"

"Yeah!" she cheered me on.

At the stoplights, I put in an order for two large pizzas to be delivered. By the time I gathered Tiana's things and got her to the condo, the delivery guy was waiting outside of the door. I unlocked it, letting her in, before grabbing the boxes from his hands.

I placed the food on the table when Tiana called out for me.

"Sydney, I have to pee!"

I rushed to the bathroom, trying to get her coat off as fast as I could. I went to unzip her pants and watched the front become soaked.

"Sorry." Tiana covered her eyes with her face.

"It's ok." I pulled her hands from her eyes. "Nothing to be ashamed about. It was an accident, ok?"

She nodded with her lip poked out. I got her wet clothes off and ran her some bath water. She begged to wash herself. Carnage usually didn't let her, but I allowed her to. I did another wash behind her, telling her each step, so that she would know how to do it. After drying her off and getting her in her pajamas, we were finally able to eat. We sat in the living room and watched *Matilda* while we ate.

Carnage came through the door, and my world stopped. I could hear my heart beating from the look on his face. He didn't say anything; he just looked at me until Tiana jumped from her chair.

"Hi, daddy!" She ran to him and wrapped her arms around his legs the best she could.

He scooped her up, kissing her cheek. "Hey, Ma Ma. You smell good." He snuggled his nose into her neck, and she giggled, trying to get away from him.

I felt like I was being punished when he didn't acknowledge me. I turned away, eating my pizza. I didn't want to look at him. Just as I settled in my feelings, he placed a kiss to my cheek. "What's up?"

"Hey." I tried not to smile, but I couldn't help it.

"Daddy," Tiana said, as he placed her down so she could finish her food. "Sydney hit the lady with the yellow sign today." She bit into her pizza.

I cringed. I knew she was a little snitch.

"I know. I heard all about it. That wasn't very nice, was it?" He grabbed a slice of pizza, eyeing me, taking a seat next to me.

"The lady's son was pulling my coat!"

"Oh, yeah?"

"Yeah. So, so, so, Sydney, she pushed him, and his mama was talking crazy to her!" Tiana defended me, and I burst into laughter.

"Talking crazy?" Carnage raised his eyebrows, and my laughter stopped immediately.

"Yeah, that's what Auntie Shany say. When people talk crazy, you pop them. Like this." She popped her father in the mouth to show him.

"Well, let's not listen to Auntie Shany, ok?"

"Ok, Daddy, but Sydney had my back today."

Now Carnage and I were both laughing.

"She did, huh?"

"Yep." Tiana nodded her head, wiping her mouth with a napkin before taking a sip of her juice.

"Well, let's get this homework done. It's bedtime soon," Carnage said before grabbing another slice of pizza.

I grabbed her book bag, bringing it over to the couch. She kneeled down on the floor in between the two of us. She spread every paper in her bookbag across the coffee table. We helped her with her homework before Carnage announced it was bedtime. She refused to go unless we both put her to bed. I stayed behind and read a book to her. I picked a book that was on the longer side, and she fell asleep before it was finished.

I left her room and found Carnage in our bed, watching the news. I expected him to give me a lecture about my actions at the school, but he was focused on the news as he was most days. I hated the news but gave it a try to see what he was so enamored with.

"Fifty-seven-year-old Ronald Peterson was found floating beside his car. Onlookers say that Peterson's car rode into a crowd at the Inner Harbor earlier this afternoon. We spoke to one of the onlookers; here's what they had to say." The video changed to a girl who looked to be barely over eighteen.

"It was crazy. We heard this horn honking crazy like. The man was screaming that his brakes weren't working. I guess he was trying to warn us. I've never seen anything like it in my life."

"When EMTs pulled his body from the car, it was discovered that the seatbelt was jammed, as well as the window lock and the brake line was torn. His death has been ruled a homicide. If you have any information, please reach out to law enforcement immediately," the news lady said.

"Crazy situation. Fox news in Maryland sends their condolences to the family of Mr. Peterson," the male reporter said.

"Did you do that?" I couldn't help myself. It was the only thing that would explain his obsession with the news.

"I did. Mr. Peterson was a bad person." He turned the TV off.

"What did he do?" I asked, curious to what Carnage deemed as bad.

"He raped a woman when he was in college."

"Oh."

"So, what happened at the school today?" He jumped topics as if what he said was regular.

I explained to him what happened, detail for detail. His face remained still the entire time.

"I'm sorry. I just saw her face when he was pulling her, and I couldn't control myself." I wiped my tears. I don't know what I was crying for.

"I don't think I need to tell you that you can't go around beating people up on school property. Thankfully, it happened so fast, I don't think anyone caught it on camera. The school isn't going to press charges, but you're banned from the school. Can't pick Tiana up or drop her off anymore. No field trips, bake sales, school plays, nothing."

That was a relief. I hated to have to miss out on those things, but I couldn't deal with another courtroom, especially not after arguing with my parents about me being a mature adult, able to make my own decisions. I would look stupid.

"How'd you make that happen?"

"A large donation. Money can get you out of everything unless I'm the reaper." He moved my hair from my face.

"And the lady I hit?"

"She's not pressing charges either."

"You paid her too?" I asked.

"No." Carnage gave me a deep stare, letting me know he'd done worse. "That was different, so it was handled differently. Her son was putting his hands on my daughter at the end of the day, and I made sure she knew it could never happen again," Carnage shrugged.

I laid on his chest. "I let my emotions get the best of me today."

"You did good today. The teacher told me you told the boy's mom that her son had hit your daughter."

"That's how it felt."

"That's how it was supposed to feel. As long as you love my daughter, I got you forever." Carnage lifted my chin, kissing me.

I'd never felt more protected than I did in that moment. Even when I was wrong, Carnage had me. I felt I was safe enough to vent to him.

"I'm homesick. When you're not here, I feel lonely," I confessed.

"I don't know if it will help, but I'll go see my family tomorrow. Let them know when we're going to meet them. Okay?" He asked and I nodded. "In the meantime, you can find a hobby. Work on your shoe line."

"I can still have my shoe line?" I jumped from his chest.

"Yeah, you can't be the face, but you can have it. In fact, I hate the sound of heels clicking, especially in my line of work. You think you can design a silent heel?" He looked over at me.

"Hell yeah. I mean, I can try." I snuggled back into his chest, getting excited.

This was the first night I was going to sleep, feeling like I was apart of Carnage and Tiana's lives. They both protected me, and I stopped at nothing to protect Tiana today. I felt like I belonged. I was going to sleep with a peaceful heart.

"Find somebody else." I stood from the kitchen island.

"Who else can do some shit this big?" Shany asked me.

"I don't know, but I can't," I shrugged.

"Carnage! This shit is not a fucking joke. Three million. Do you really want to put that type of money, that big of a kill in someone else's hands?" Josie asked me.

The whole point of me working so hard all those years was to be done with killing. I found a way to maintain my urge and didn't need to do these long drawn-out jobs. The money wasn't as enticing and hadn't been for years. I made more than enough money off the kills everyone else did. The risk wasn't worth it, outside of the fact that my wife had just complained about feeling lonely.

"How long is the job again?" I asked.

"Three days tops," Josie answered.

That was closer to a week because I needed a day to become someone else and at least two to decompress. They took more time, but they held me over longer than the petty local kills. I could do this shit, get it over with, and come home to give Sydney my undivided attention.

"Aight. Give me the run down." I leaned back in my chair, focusing on Shany and Josie's words.

"Alejandro and Alexander Perez, twins in New York. They

run a night club called Tranquilo. Like most clubs, they ran drugs throughout the club. Apparently, a billionaire's daughter overdosed in their club. He wants them both dead. They're surrounded by security guards at all times, and there's no address on them." Josie filled me in.

"I figure you could use the first day to visit the club, feel it out. Second day, find an address, figure out their daily moves, get Geppetto to hack their schedules, and on day three make your move and get the fuck outta there," Shany suggested.

"I don't need you to tell me how to do my job. How many people you killed?" I asked her. I knew the answer was none.

"Oh, this must be about me not liking your little wife. Well, I looked her up on social media, and she looks like the typical bougie IG model. I like her even less now. I can't believe you, of all niggas, pressed about this attention craving bitch."

I ran my hands down my face. "Shany, I will fuck you up in here. When I get back from this job, me *and* my wife are stopping by. All that attitude shit better be dealt with 'cause I have no problem embarrassing you."

"Yayy," Josie clapped her hands. "I can't wait to meet her."

"You a fucking clown." Shany shook her head at Josie.

"I'm supposed to be mad 'cause you are? You act like Carnage is your boyfriend and not your brother. You talk about the rest of us, but you're more codependent on him than any of us. She's clearly not going anywhere, so you might as well get over it."

"Fuck both of y'all," Shany said, leaving the room.

"You could've handled this better, Carnage. You know how she gets about you." Josie poured herself a glass of water.

"She just gave a whole speech about us catering to Mommy and her issues. Is that not the same shit?" I extended my arm in the direction Shany stormed off in.

"I'm just saying," Josie shrugged.

"Say that shit to somebody else. I don't want to hear it." I got up, leaving Josie standing in the kitchen. "Make sure somebody picks Tiana up from school today. She can stay here until I get back." I slammed the door behind me.

Shany was a big ass baby. One minute she was a gangsta. The next, she was whining and complaining about some shit. I stayed out of their relationships. I wasn't that overbearing big or little brother. As long as a nigga didn't put his hands on either of them, I didn't give a fuck. Shany was always in my fucking business. Even when it came to Nia, Simone, whatever the fuck, she was always in my shit.

I called Camille in the car.

"Yes, massa," she answered on the first ring as always.

"You still mad, I see." I pulled out of my mother's driveway.

"Massa, I don't know what you're talking about. I'm just being a good little slave."

"Camille!"

"Carnage!"

"What was I supposed to do? My *wife* doesn't want you to have a key to her home. Was I supposed to tell her no?"

"I would feel the same way if it were my husband, but I'm still mad."

"Well, I'm sorry. Maybe she'll come around. I need a new spot, though. I got a job and I need somewhere to decompress. I'm not going to Nesha's for that long; I can't relax there. Have you been checking in on her?" I asked.

"Sure have, place is still spotless. I saw Ariel playing

outside, and her clothes were clean. Paying one of the teenagers out there to monitor her shit on the low. She ain't had no male visitors except hair clients. I can't promise she's not fucking them, but they're not staying the night or anything."

"Cool. I'm thinking something in the cut. Nothing flashy but also nothing that would make me a sore thumb if I pull up in my truck. No nosey ass neighbors.

"Well, nosey neighbors are everywhere, Carnage. Everyone wants to know who the fuck is living near them."

"Well, no nosey neighbors that'll call the police about suspicious activity."

"I'll see what I can do. When do you leave? You need me to book you a flight?"

"Nah. I'm going to drive, so I can get into character. New York ain't but a minute away."

"Cool, anything else?"

"Can you tell Sydney for me?"

"Ha! Hell. No. That's all you; I don't want no parts of that attitude."

"I was joking. But I do need you to make sure she's good while I'm gone. She mentioned being lonely."

"I'm not fitna go kick it with her ass, but I'll check in every few hours."

"That's all I ask. Thank you."

"You're welcome. Bye, nigga." Camille hung up on me.

A woman like Camille was rare. She wanted me for herself but pushed me towards Sydney. She was pissed at me for taking her key but was still doing whatever I asked. Yeah, it was her job, but she could quit if she wanted. With her skills, she could convince a motherfucker to hire her. Camille was down for me. Maybe a little of that could rub off on Sydney. Not that she wasn't for me, but she didn't trust me. I could tell by all her questions. She always needed to know why. One day, the why wouldn't meet her standards. I didn't know where we would stand when that day came.

I sat in our parking garage, scared to tell her that I would be leaving. In a few hours, no less. Again, I was experiencing things I hadn't before. I'd never had to seek approval or even let anyone know my whereabouts. This was different. Outside of my parents, I didn't fear shit, but I'd be lying if I said I wasn't scared as fuck of Sydney. The fear of her leaving me was sitting on my chest. I searched my head for any way out of it, but I was stuck. I had to go in here and tell the truth.

Walking to the elevator and taking the ride to the floor of our condo, I lost my charm. A nigga's swag dipped out on him. My shoulders tightened as I walked into the apartment.

"Hey, baby." Sydney smiled at me.

I wiped my hands on my shirt, feeling they were sweaty. My legs wanted to run.

"Hey, babe." I leaned over to kiss her, and she pulled away.

"What you do?" She rolled her eyes, pushing me away.

"How you figure I did something?" I was curious as to what my tell was. I thought I was well composed.

"Because not once in our entire marriage, abortion fiasco, or Cabo adventure have you ever called me babe." She crossed her arms.

Damn. She had me shook if I was slipping like that.

I scratched the back of my neck. "I gotta work."

"Ok?" Sydney stretched the word, waiting for more.

My throat was burning. I felt like I was about to explain to my mother why I did some dumb shit. "For a few days."

"Carnage!"

"I know, man."

I leaned against the edge of the wall between the living room and the hallway. I put my hands under my arms and a foot against the wall.

"Days?" Sydney's eyes watered.

"You can meet my family the second I get back, and you will never have to go through this lonely shit again, I swear." I threw my arms up.

"Tiana is staying with your family?" she asked.

I nodded my head. "Yeah. It's days, so…"

"Okay," Sydney nodded, sitting on one of her legs and unmuting the TV.

"It'll go by fast; I promise." I leaned down in front of the couch, moving her hair from her face.

"Yeah, for you. You out playing superhero. I'm home, doing nothing. No family. No friends. I have nothing when you and Tiana leave," her eyes watered. Her lips were tight. I felt like shit.

"I didn't think about it like that," I shook my head.

"I'm sure," she wiped her eyes.

"When I get back—"

"Tell me when you get back," Sydney cut me off.

I thought it'd be best to leave her alone. I took what I had on me and headed for the door.

"I love you, Sydney." I looked her way with my hand on the door.

"I love you, too," she mumbled, not bothering to look at me.

When I got home, I was going to make it up to her. I'd use my decompression time to find a way to make this shit work for her. I was not willing to lose Sydney over some shit in my control.

It was 7 p.m. and I had already been drinking for three hours. I sang Mary J. Blige's "Seven Days" loudly while holding a picture of Carnage. The song didn't apply, but it counted the days of the week, and that was all my sad ass was doing, counting the days my husband had been gone. Two days and two nights. I wasn't even smart enough to get stroked down before he left. I was in this bitch sad, drunk, and horny. He called me every morning and every night from a burner phone. I think that's what he called it. The phone rang, throwing me off my vibe.

I saw Tiana's name on the screen. My heart did a pitter patter, happy she thought of me, but also happy to hear a real person's voice.

"Hello?"

"Good night, Sydney!" Tiana's voice chimed, and my heart melted.

"Good night, Tiana. Thanks for calling me."

As I pulled the phone away from my ear to hang up, I heard another voice say hello.

"Hello?" I asked, confused.

"Hi, honey. This is Carnage's mom. How are you?" she asked.

I sat up, trying to force myself sober. "I—I'm fine," I stuttered. "And you?"

"I'm well. You know you've made quite the impression on my granddaughter."

"Have I?" I couldn't hold my smile in.

"She harassed me to call her father to get your number for her. She couldn't go another night without saying good night to you. You've been in her bedtime prayers every night and Sydney this and Sydney that," she laughed.

"She has made quite the impression on me as well. I adore Tiana. She's made this transition easier." I cringed at my confession.

"Well, we have something in common because she's just pulled me out of something heavy, too. I guess we have us an angel baby."

"You might be right," I laughed with her.

"Well, I know Carnage said he'd introduce us when he returned, but how about I send you the address and you stop by tomorrow?" she offered.

My heart stopped. I forgot how to use my words. I wanted to say hell yeah because I didn't have a thing going on without my man. The pit of my stomach told me to say no. Carnage said he'd do it when he got back. I had to trust him. I had to move past my insecurities.

"Well, I guess we'll go on and wait for Carnage then." His mother got tired of waiting for me to respond.

"I think that's best."

"Well, have a good night, Ms. Sydney."

"You too, Mrs. Essex."

I ended the call. I beamed from ear to ear. I wasn't sure if that was a test, but I passed that motherfucker. It was nice to hear from his mom. I couldn't stop smiling about finally being able to talk to Tiana because I missed her.

It wasn't long before Carnage called to tell me good night.

"Hi, husband! I'm drunk."

"I know. My mother told me," Carnage laughed.

"Oh, my God." I leaned forward on the couch, pulling my hair. "I am so embarrassed."

"Don't be. Nothing she hasn't heard before. You good, though. I hear you in there, drinking and I'm lying if I say I'm not a little worried about you."

"Yeah, I get it. But, I'm fine. I'm just drinking to entertain myself not to hide pain."

"Just checking. I miss you."

"I miss you, too, baby. I can't wait for you and Tiana to get home. I was so happy to hear her voice. I might miss her more than I miss you," I laughed lightly.

"Yeah? Then I guess I can take my time getting home."

"Don't you dare," I said through gritted teeth.

"Never. I'm anxious to get back to you," Carnage said, making me smile. "But I was calling to say good night."

"So early?" I peeked at the clock. He usually called me later than eight.

"Yeah, I gotta make a move. I love you."

"I love you, too."

I must have dozed off because I almost jumped out of my skin when there was a knock at the door. I hesitated on getting up until they knocked again. "DoorDash!"

I didn't remember ordering shit. There was no telling what I'd done in my drunkenness. I slid on some pajama pants over my booty shorts. I was already in a hoodie and didn't have to worry about my titties.

"Thank you," I answered the door.

"Welcome." The older man looked at me.

I used my foot to hold the door in place as he handed me my drink.

"Have a good night." I turned to let the door close behind me but instead fell to my face from my leg being pulled. "Shit."

"Shut the fuck up." One of the men stood over me, putting something heavy against the back of my head.

The other man taped my hands together. One turned me around by my legs and dragged me over to the floor in front of the couch. I watched the other guy lock the door.

"I'm going to say this one time." He held up his pointer finger. "I just need you to answer a few questions. If you try to scream, I'm going to shoot you in your head." He aimed his gun.

I nodded, taking a hard swallow. "I understand."

I couldn't stop the tears that poured down my face. My husband was a real-life superhero, but I knew he wouldn't make it in time to save me from this.

"Ok. Where is your husband?"

"I don't know," I answered honestly. My heart was in my stomach. My legs shook in fear.

"I don't like being lied to."

"J doesn't tell me anything. What did he do?" I didn't know what I was stalling for, but I was trying what I could.

"J?"

"Yes," I nodded. "That's my husband."

The guys looked at each other. The one that'd been silent, hit me across the face with an open hand.

"So, you don't know your husband's name is Carnage?" he asked me.

"Carnage?" I pretended to be confused. "My husband's name is J. Whatever you think he did, he didn't. You have the wrong man."

"Nah. We got the right nigga and the right bitch." He yanked me up by my hair.

I tired to stay quiet, but the pain that shot through my scalp was excruciating.

"Tape this bitch's mouth shut," the one holding my head ordered.

"You gon' talk." He grabbed at my booty shorts. "One way or the—"

The fire alarm in the building sounded off. The guys looked at each other. In one motion, they cut through the tape on my hands before disappearing out of the apartment.

Thankfully, I still had my pajama pants on. I slid into my slides before rushing out of the house. I felt for whoever's apartment was on fire. Hopefully, no one was too injured, but if they were, they'd saved my life.

We stood outside for nearly an hour before the fire department let us back in the building. There was never a fire. This shit was freaking me out, and Carnage wasn't answering his phone. I hated to do it, but I called Camille. She answered on the first ring.

Carnage

I figured since I was out of town, I'd might as well go hard. I was covered in plastic from head to toe, wearing a gas mask, and black latex gloves. It wasn't often I was able to go all out like this. I grabbed the twins up separately. No one carries security 24/7. I grabbed Alexander coming out of his side chick's house. I grabbed Alejandro when he was leaving a doctor's appointment. Shit was easy.

Currently, they were both tied up to chairs, bound by their forearms and legs. One was crying while the other was taking their last breath. Since I grabbed them a day earlier than planned, I had time to experiment and ease my stress. I wanted to see how long it would take for Alexander to die if I drilled into his chest without hitting any major arteries.

I hated drug dealers. I didn't respect their hustle. They weren't legit to me. They ain't have to go out there and get it; their customers came to them. All they had to do was hand off some drugs, and they couldn't do it without getting caught.

Blood splattered as I cut straight down the center of his chest like I was cutting a slice of cake. His scream echoed around the warehouse. One hour and six minutes. That's how long it took.

"Please. I'll give you anything!" Alejandro cried.

"There's nothing I can do. You brought this on yourself. You know someone put three mil on your head? That's a lot of money. If it wasn't me, it would've been someone. I wasn't going to let anyone else have money that belonged to me."

I was talking my shit because I hadn't decided how I wanted to kill him yet.

Sydney had been calling. I hadn't grabbed my phone, but I heard her ringtone. Answering would be a distraction, just the ringing of my phone was doing enough damage to my concentration. I knew she was drunk and ain't want shit forreal. Hearing her plead for me to come home and fuck her horniness away wasn't what I needed right now.

"Just kill me already!" Alejandro cried.

Camille's ringtone went off, and I went over to my phone. She knew not to call me on a job. So, if she was calling, it was important.

"Hello?"

"You need to get home, like yesterday."

"On my way," I hung up.

"Well, looks like it's your lucky day." I smiled at Alejandro before shooting him in the head. He got a quicker death than his brother and could go be with him.

I stripped out of the plastic covering over my clothes. I kept my gloves on until getting in my car. I pulled them off, folding one into the other. When I was far enough down the highway, I tossed them over the bridge. Driving seemed like the better option when considering the process of getting a ticket and waiting for a flight. So, I sped down the highway.

Sydney was calling again, and I thought to ignore it. I wasn't sure if she was the emergency. If she wasn't, I didn't want to scare her.

"Hello?"

"Carnage, finally!"

"I'm sorry. I'm on my way home now. I need to focus on driving. Stay up. I'm coming." I hung up before she could protest.

I needed to decompress. To do that, I needed silence. I knew that I needed to rush home but in my head, I was still a murderous nigga, needing to take out the twins I'd already killed. If I didn't separate myself from the job I'd just done, anybody could get it.

When I saw the welcome to Maryland sign, I got off the exit and parked. I called Camille back.

"What happened?" I asked when she answered.

"Sydney said some niggas came in there looking for you, tied her up, and put a gun to her head."

I sat silently. Ain't no random nigga learned my address. My mind drifted to who could be looking for me. I always killed the witnesses, except Tiana. Maybe she had more family that Nia/Simone didn't tell me about.

"Did she say anything else?"

"Just that she got away when the fire alarm went off."

"Bet." I hung up.

The fire alarm was all I needed to know. I slid back into traffic, calling Sydney from the car.

"Carnage, where are you?"

"I'll be there in thirty minutes." It was supposed to take forty-five, but I knew I'd could speed it up. "Get dressed. Meet me in the garage."

"Carnage, what is going on?" I could hear her moving around to do as I said.

"Thirty minutes, baby."

"Ok."

Like I said, I got to the condo in thirty minutes. I watched Sydney get off the elevator. I was at the passenger door, waiting to open it. Sydney rushed me for a hug. I could feel her body shaking, so I squeezed her tight. I knew exactly what happened and knew she was never in any real danger, but she needed to be comforted.

"Get in the car." I kissed her forehead.

She climbed in, and I shut the door behind her, taking my seat at the wheel.

"Where are we going?" she asked as I pulled out of the parking garage.

"A victim lineup."

"You mean a police lineup?"

"I'm not the police. Imma round some niggas up, you gon' point out the motherfuckers that played with you, and they gon' be fucking victims."

"And then what? You're going to kill them?" Sydney asked.

"Yes."

Sydney went quiet. I could see her leg shaking out of the corner of my eye.

"Are you ok with that?"

"I mean, they won't be able to see me, right? I don't have to stand in front of them. I mean, if there's no glass in between—"

I hit the brakes in the middle of the street as the cars behind me honked their horns and went around.

"You can stay in the car. You can point them out behind the tint in the windows. I'd rather you trust me to protect you and stand in front of them niggas and point them out. But whatever you're comfortable with."

"I trust you but putting your car in park in the middle of the street makes me think I shouldn't," Sydney nodded her head.

"It don't feel like you do." I put the car in drive and pulled off.

"I trust you. I'm just more comfortable behind the tint." Sydney opened her phone and began scrolling.

I wasn't going to push her out of her comfort zone, no matter how bad I wanted her to trust me. She needed to know I had her if she was ever going to be comfortable in Maryland. It always felt like, at any minute, she was going to jump on a plane, and I'd never see her again.

We pulled up in front of the spot that housed a bunch of bum ass niggas who would jump at the chance to get on with me. Dumb ass niggas who took dumb ass orders from my dumb ass sister, thinking they were doing work for me.

I knocked on the door. I didn't look back at the car, but I could feel Sydney's eyes on me.

"What's up, Carnage?" One young boy held his hand out for dap.

"Fuck all that. I need all you niggas out here now." I waved my gun, directing him to take his ass in the house.

"Bet." Dude went back in to get the rest of them.

Seven niggas came piling out of the house. Only two looked like they knew I was there for them. I didn't even need Sydney to point them out.

"Which two of you niggas thought it was cool to run in my shit? Who the fuck thought that was a good idea?"

One nigga cleared his throat. "Shany said she had a job. I took the job. She said she was testing your bitch—"

I didn't hesitate to shoot him. He dropped, and they made

space for his body by sliding out of the way.

"Where the other nigga at?"

"I don't know which one of you niggas did that shit, but y'all better speak the fuck up!" The nigga who answered the door barked on the other five. "I'm not fitna be laying on the ground like this nigga because your pussy ass did some dumb shit."

Normally, I didn't like to be interrupted, but I let it slide. Whatever got me closer to my mission. He was the only one who knew I didn't have a problem shooting until they were all dead.

I heard the car door open but didn't turn around.

"It was that one." Sydney came to me and pointed the nigga out.

"That one, baby?"

"Mhmm," she nodded.

"Y'all see her? That's my fucking wife." I flashed my ring. "None of that bullshit boyfriend, girlfriend. My wife!"

The dudes nodded their heads, understanding. Sydney leaned against the side of the car. My wife looked good as a motherfucker. She was converting to the bad side better than I expected.

"Yo, Carnage." The nigga held his arms up. "I did what Shany asked me."

"He grabbed my leg, and I fell to my face. He held a gun to my head."

"Shany asked us to scare her to see if she would give you up. She didn't."

"I know she didn't. You two stupid motherfuckers crossed me, and then snitched on my sister."

The nigga took off running, and the dude who answered

the door shot him. I gave him a head nod.

"Let this be a lesson for all you niggas. If you don't want nobody knocking on your mama's door with bad news, stay the fuck in line! Shany is not the motherfucking boss, and she not fitna let none of you niggas hit 'cause you did her a favor. I'm the fucking boss! Clean this shit up," I grilled them, tucking my gun.

I opened the door for Sydney, shutting it behind her, before getting in myself and pulling off.

"You ok?" I asked, pulling into the street.

"Yeah. I feel energized. Let's go home and fuck." She leaned over, kissing on my neck.

"I'm wit' all that, after we deal with my sister. I hope you're ready to meet the family."

That shit was so motherfucking sexy. I was sitting in a pool of my own juices. I felt vindicated as I sat in the car and heard the first shot ring off. My husband did that shit for me. I wanted to give him all of me right there on the sidewalk. I didn't pull that trigger, but it gave me the confidence to get out of the car and point that nigga out.

Now that we were parked in front of his family's house, a bitch was shook. I thought we'd discuss a plan of action on the way over here, but Carnage hadn't said a word.

He got out of the car. I followed, assuming he expected me to be right behind him. When we walked up the steps, his keys jingled in his hands. It was the only sound I could focus on, outside of my heart trying to beat through my chest.

He turned the key, snatching my hand as if my body wasn't attached. He pulled his phone out, sending a text, pissed off.

"Sit down." He pointed to a chair. I quickly took a seat. He was madder than he was when he had killed those guys outside. "You want something to drink?" He pulled a water out for himself, then looked to me.

"Yeah, water is fine."

"Oh, shit." A girl I assumed to be his sister walked into the kitchen.

"Josie, this is my wife, Sydney. Sydney, this is my baby sister, Josie. Sit down." He pointed Josie into a chair.

"Nice to meet you." Josie smiled and waved.

"Nice to finally meet you too." I extended the same smile to her.

"What the fuck is she doing here?"

"Shany, this is my wife, Sydney. Sydney, this is the bitch who played with you earlier."

"Bitch? I'm not scared of you, Carnage. We can fight, my nigga."

"Shany, go the fuck head before I really do you bad in here."

"You better find some respect!" Shany was mugging my husband.

I was trying to be the supportive wife, the bridge between what was going on with my husband and his sister, but I wasn't a fan. It wasn't even what she did to me. It was just her. Her energy was ugly, like murky water.

"Respect?! Shany, you had motherfuckers in my shit to get at my wife!"

"I told them not to hurt her!" Shany argued.

My blood boiled, looking at her. She set me up. I passed her bullshit test, but them niggas looked like they were going to rape me had the fire alarm not gone off. My hands shook with anger. I didn't want to hit her, but I wasn't sure I'd be able to control myself.

"I don't give a fuck!" Carnage yelled, pushing his sister to the floor.

I jumped out of my seat. I didn't know what to do. I was settled with my husband jumping to my defense but not at the expense of me having any type of relationship with his family.

"Carnage, let's just go."

"Fuck that!" he yelled at me, and I backed up.

"What is all this gahdamn noise?" I recognized his mother's voice from our brief phone call. She was pretty. Didn't look a day over thirty.

"Carnage just pushed me." Shany started making her way off the floor.

"Tell her what the fuck you did, Shany!" Carnage yelled.

"Somebody better tell me the who, what, where, when, and why right now!"

"Shany think she's fucking daddy! She pulled one of his setups on my fucking wife! Shit went horribly wrong!"

"How did it go wrong?" Shany slapped her hands together. "Your little Barbie is fine and well, and she passed the test," Shany shrugged.

"Because I killed them niggas. Both of them. Getting my hands dirty on some stupid shit."

"You what? Hutch and Drummer?" Shany's eyes watered.

"Yup. Both of them niggas." Carnage formed his fingers into a gun, demonstrating how he killed them. I was the only one laughing at his pettiness.

"They didn't deserve that. They weren't ready for no shit like that. That's why I sent them to do this petty shit."

"You shouldn't have had them on the street at all! They shouldn't have been in my shit!"

"Everybody, relax." My mother-in-law threw her hands up, stepping between them.

In a split second, Shany grabbed a knife, trying to move around her mother, and now Josie. I felt sick to my stomach. There was too much going on at once. I rushed to the kitchen sink and threw up everything in my stomach.

"Oh, my God. I'm so sorry." My face heated in embarrassment. I threw up in these people's sink.

"Don't you worry about that, sweetheart. Are you feeling okay?" His mother came over and rubbed my back, passing me a napkin.

"What, is she pregnant too?" Shany huffed.

"Daddy?" I heard a tired Tiana's small voice.

"Hey, Ma Ma. You want to go home with Daddy?"

"Yes. Are you okay, Sydney?"

I wiped any residue from my lips before turning to face her. "Yup. Just a little upset tummy. I'm okay." I forced a smile. I wanted to lay down, immediately.

"We outta here." Carnage began walking, and I tossed a wave to his mom and Josie. "Let me be clear," he stopped, turning around, "Sydney is my wife. That's what the fuck it is. Stop fucking playing with me, Shany." He started walking, and I kept up, despite feeling like I needed a bed.

There was a silent ride to the house that consisted of Carnage rubbing my thighs. I appreciated the small comforts he provided. We walked through the doors, and it felt like home. Carnage put Tiana to sleep, and I took my black ass to the bedroom. I passed out before he made it to the bed.

"Sydney." I opened my eyes from Carnage shaking me. "I'm going to drop Tiana off at school. Be ready when I get back. I'm taking you to breakfast. Shopping. Whatever you want." He kissed my cheek before I felt Tiana's small lips too.

"See you later, Sydney," Tiana laughed.

"Have a good day at school."

When the front door shut, I rolled over, spreading my arms for a morning stretch. I jumped in the shower, trying to wash away the mess from the night before. I found myself smiling at my husband stepping about me to any and everybody. He didn't play about me. I'd never had that in my man before. It was the most secure space I'd ever rested in.

When he came back, I met him in the garage and as promised, he took me to breakfast. When he suggested Waffle House, I jumped at the chance to have it again. We'd only gotten in one bite before his mother called, demanding that both of us come back to the house while Tiana was in school. Carnage was in no rush and wanted to stay to finish our food. When he got tired of me sitting there with my arms folded, he got us to-go boxes. He left a tip, and we left. I finished my food in the car and tried to feed him his, but he insisted that he wasn't hungry anymore. He was just as spoiled as I was.

The speech could've been used before getting out of the car last night. Instead, he had a speech now.

"When we go in here, just let me handle it." He got out of the car.

"I don't need you to speak for me," I told him when he opened my door.

"When did I say that?"

"That's basically what you saying." I moved passed him, walking up the steps before him, like I was a regular visitor.

On the platform, Carnage unlocked the door, letting me in.

"This shit is crazy," Shany said under her breath, but we all heard her.

"Good afternoon." I smiled at Josie and my mother-in-law, ignoring Shany completely.

"Heyyy," Josie waved.

"Hi, sweetie."

"What's up, Ma?" Carnage hugged his mother, giving her a kiss on the cheek.

"Hey, baby."

"What's this about?" Carnage took a seat and pulled my body next to his.

"I just figured we needed a proper introduction, a calm one." His mother took a sip from her coffee mug.

"I don't have anything to say to him until he apologizes for putting his hands on me." Shany was in the chair, arms folded and pouting like a child.

"Then, we'll never talk again." Carnage took a sip of his water.

"Carnage!" his mother eyed him.

"Man, I don't have time for this." He looked at his watch.

I couldn't care less about him not fucking with his sister, but what he wasn't going to do was talk to his mother like that in front of me. I slapped his leg, and he pulled it away fast.

"Shany, apologize to your brother and his wife."

"I don't want that shit, Ma. Too little, too late. She had niggas run in my shit. Why is everybody acting like I'm tripping?" he stood, looking around the room. "You mad that I pushed you? Be grateful I didn't shoot your dumb ass."

"Carnage!" His mom, Josie, and I stood up at the same time.

"See what he does when he gets a new bitch?"

Something took over me, and I grabbed his water bottle from his hands and flung it at Shany's face, before leaping over the coffee table. I only got one hit before Carnage was grabbing me from her.

"I did nothing to her! I was almost raped, and now she's calling me a bitch! I'm done. If this is how your family is, I'm out. I don't want this." I talked shit as he carried me out of the door. He put me in the car.

"I'm sorry." We sat in silence. He hadn't even turned the car on yet.

"You didn't do anything," I shrugged, mad at the world.

"I could've prepared my family better than what I did. Word is my bond, though. My sister will never play with you like that again." Carnage kissed me while turning the car on.

I nodded my head, not saying anything. I was disappointed in myself for showing my ass in front of his mother, but the bitch had nerve. I remained as calm as I could. I wasn't allowing her to talk to me crazy when just a few hours before, she was trying to have me raped. Fuck her. We never had to have a relationship if it was up to me.

Camille called. Carnage put his phone in privacy, holding it to his hear.

"What's up?"

I'm not sure what she said to him, but it made him step on the gas to take me home. Just me, because he dropped me off in the parking garage, not even making sure I made it safely inside of our condo. He told me he would tell me about it when he got home. There was always something going on. Never a moment of peace.

Shany's voice was annoying. Carnage prepared me that his sister dressed like a stud, but she liked men. What he didn't tell me was that her voice was high pitched like a fucking bird chirping at five a.m. Her calling me a bitch and asking if I was pregnant was the only thing that replayed from all of the bullshit she spoke.

I still wasn't familiar with the roads and feared going out alone and getting lost. I remembered there was a pregnancy test stuffed into one of my pink purses. It was apart of me manifesting a daughter when I was with Kyle. Damn. I guess I aborted the daughter I manifested.

My things were still untouched. I hated unpacking. I found the boxes marked *bedroom closet*. There were two large moving boxes. I rummaged through them, looking for my purses. When I found them, I searched through the pink purse I was certain it was in. I pulled it out, setting it to the side. You'd think I'd start putting things away, but I stuffed everything back in its box, taping it like it was never opened.

I searched the box for an expiration date. Seeing it was still good to go, I grabbed one of the gallons of water and the test, walked into the bathroom, and locked the door.

Carnage

Camille only called to tell me that Ariel called her, saying it was an emergency. I was glad I had Camille doing check ins because with all this shit going on, I couldn't promise I would have answered Ariel's calls. I tried calling Camille back several times but got no answer. I used my key, getting into the apartment.

Nesha stood in the center of the room, holding a gun to her head.

"Nesha. What the fuck?" I put my hands on my head.

"I don't want to do this shit anymore. I'm tired. All I want is someone to love me."

"Your daughter loves you, Nesha. I love you." I walked closer.

"No, you don't, and you killed the only person who did!" she stomped.

"He didn't love you. That's not love. Love is healing, not painful. It is calm, patient, and warmth. Is that what he felt like?" I tried to take a few more steps closer, and she shooed me back with her gun.

"Nesha, please. At least let me take Ariel out of here," Camille begged.

"That's probably a good idea." She brushed her hair back. "Yeah, yeah. Give mommy a hug, baby." She reached her arms out for Ariel.

Ariel looked to me to see if it was okay. I nodded my head.

Nesha did stupid shit, but I didn't feel she'd kill her daughter. I wasn't sure that she wouldn't shoot herself once Ariel was out of the room. I struggled with keeping Ariel here to prevent her mother from firing that gun or letting her leave with Camille so she wouldn't have to see it, if she did.

"Mommy loves you, ok? But mommy is sad." Nesha wiped tears from Ariel's eyes.

"Do I make you sad, mommy?" Ariel sniffed.

"No, no, no, baby. Love. Love makes mommy sad. You are the best thing that's ever happened to me, okay? I just don't want to hurt you anymore, ok?"

Her speech was getting on the heavier side. In the best interest of Ariel, I had Camille take her out of the building. Ariel screamed for her mother down the hall of the apartments. It was heart wrenching. Nesha weeped harder. In the blink of an eye, she shot herself. Her body fell and unfortunately, I had to get the fuck out of there.

I met Camille at a McDonald's. After she got some food in her, Camille would break the news to Ariel because she said I wasn't empathetic enough and would only make things worse.

"Does she have any family?" We stood outside of Camille's car while Ariel ate in the backseat.

"A grandmother," I told her.

"Well, I'll make contact with her. See if she can come get her or if we need to take her to her."

"Nesha's mother is not a good person."

"So, what do you suggest we do?"

I thought about it. The only thing that made sense to me was for me to take her. I was her godfather.

"No, Carnage. I know that look." Camille shook her head at

me. "You have enough newness going on."

"It's the only way I'll know she's good."

"And Sydney?"

"She'll have to deal with it," I shrugged.

My chest tightened at the thought of Sydney not wanting to deal with it. It was a commitment I made prior to her, but I had to honor it now. If I had to take an L, I'd just have to take it.

"Well, she looks like she's done eating. I'm going to break the news to her, *gently*."

"Aight."

I waited there, beside the car. I watched Ariel burst into tears, pulling at her eyes. I jumped up, ready to spring into action, but Camille held her hand up, saying she had it. I guess children were my weakness because all I wanted to do was go back and shoot Nesha a few more times for the shit she'd done to her daughter.

Ariel looked at me and nodded her head to Camille.

She opened the car door and ran to me. I scooped her up in my arms the same way I did with Tiana. She squeezed her arms around my neck and cried into my chest. When I turned our bodies so our faces showed to Camille, her mouth dropped. I put Ariel in the car, shutting the door, preparing to take her home.

"What?" I asked Camille as she was stepping out of her car.

"How old is this little girl?" Camille asked.

"Like seven or eight. I'm not sure."

"And how long ago were you fucking with Nesha?" Camille was staring at Ariel.

I stepped back from her. "Nah." I ran my hands down my face.

"Are you one hundred percent sure?"

"I asked Nesha when she told me she was pregnant. She said there was no way she was mine."

"If you were fucking her, there's a way. Looking at the both of you, with her in your arms. I don't know. She looks just like you," Camille shook her head.

"What the fuck, man!"

"Don't scare her, stupid. Take her home, *tell* your wife what's going on, and get a DNA test and move forward from there. Im telling you, though, she's your daughter."

"Aight, man," I exhaled. "Thanks for your help today. Lifesaver."

"I don't know if that's true this time," she exhaled. "Call me and let me know what happens. Or text me if your wife allows." She gave a small laugh before waving bye to Ariel.

On the car ride to the house, I ran the dates over and over. It didn't add up to how old Ariel was supposed to be. She said Ariel was a premie and came two months early. The only way I could be her father was if she wasn't a premie and was birthed at forty weeks like she was supposed to be. Nesha would have lied to me. Again, I wanted to shoot her ass.

"Come on," I opened her door, reaching for her.

I carried her on the elevator and into the apartment.

"Baby!! I'm pregnant," Sydney smiled wide.

Sydney met me at the door, and her mouth dropped seeing Ariel in my arms.

"We need to talk. Wait. Did you say pregnant?"

Fuck. I went from one child to three in a matter of a few hours.

WANT TO INTERACT WITH T'ANN MARIE & HER TEAM? JOIN OUR READERS GROUPS ON FACEBOOK!

T'ANN MARIE PRESENTS: GRANDMA'S HOUSE | Facebook

T'ANN MARIE PRESENTS: GRANDMA'S HOUSE 2.0 | Facebook

WIN PRIZES, BE APART OF LIVE BOOK DISCUSSIONS & MORE!

Join Our Mailing List:

http://eepurl.com/gU81k5

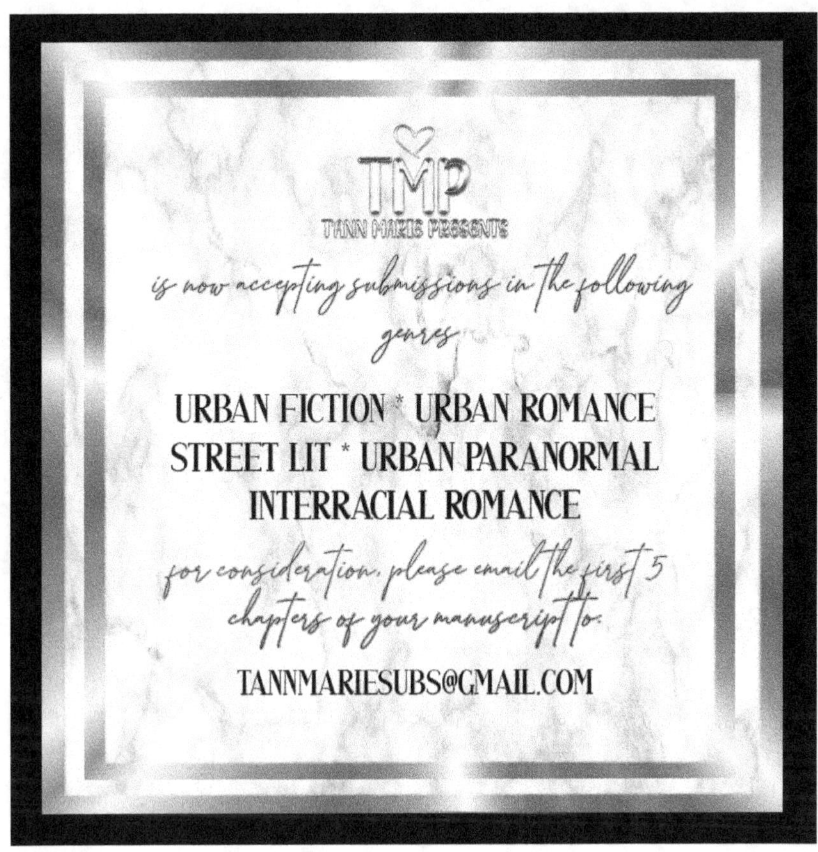

TMP
TANN MARIE PRESENTS
is now accepting submissions in the following genres

URBAN FICTION * URBAN ROMANCE
STREET LIT * URBAN PARANORMAL
INTERRACIAL ROMANCE

for consideration, please email the first 5 chapters of your manuscript to:

TANNMARIESUBS@GMAIL.COM